Forget Me Not

Aslı Eti

First published in Turkish in 2016 by Kırmızı Kedi as *Unutma Beni*
Copyright © 2018 Aslı Eti.
Translation © Feyza Howell 2016
Illustrations © Mehtap Korkmaz 2018

The rights of Aslı Eti, Feyza Howell and Mehtap Korkmaz to be identified as the author, translator and illustrator respectively of this work have been asserted by them in accordance with the Copyright, Designs and Patents Act 1988.

All rights reserved. No part of this book may be used or reproduced by any means, graphic, electronic, or mechanical, including photocopying, recording, taping or by any information storage retrieval system without the written permission of the author except in the case of brief quotations embodied in critical articles and reviews.

This is a work of fiction. All of the characters, names, incidents, organizations, and dialogue in this novel are either the products of the author's imagination or are used fictitiously.

Balboa Press books may be ordered through booksellers or by contacting:

Balboa Press
A Division of Hay House
1663 Liberty Drive
Bloomington, IN 47403
www.balboapress.com
1 (877) 407-4847

Because of the dynamic nature of the Internet, any web addresses or links contained in this book may have changed since publication and may no longer be valid. The views expressed in this work are solely those of the author and do not necessarily reflect the views of the publisher, and the publisher hereby disclaims any responsibility for them.

The author of this book does not dispense medical advice or prescribe the use of any technique as a form of treatment for physical, emotional, or medical problems without the advice of a physician, either directly or indirectly. The intent of the author is only to offer information of a general nature to help you in your quest for emotional and spiritual well-being. In the event you use any of the information in this book for yourself, which is your constitutional right, the author and the publisher assume no responsibility for your actions.

Any people depicted in stock imagery provided by Getty Images are models, and such images are being used for illustrative purposes only.
Certain stock imagery © Getty Images.

Print information available on the last page.

A catalogue record for this book is available from the British Library.

ISBN: 978-1-9822-0793-9 (sc)
ISBN: 978-1-9822-0791-5 (hc)
ISBN: 978-1-9822-0792-2 (e)

Library of Congress Control Number: 2018908063

Balboa Press rev. date: 07/19/2018

Contents

Introduction vii

1 1

2 9

3 18

4 26

5 43

6 48

7 63

8 71

9 83

10 88

11 93

12 100

13 105

14 108

About the Author 111

Introduction

Some things are meant to be understood much later.

I want to tell you an old story. One from long ago, from a land far, far away… One I had long since forgotten. The trouble is, I wasn't even aware that I had forgotten. I'm just beginning to recall now. I must have got lost amongst all that I've got to do, all the places I've got to get to. And time has obviously drawn a thick curtain over everything. Until, that is, today, when those dusty lines somehow turned up out of the blue… I was wiping my bookcase when that old manuscript floated down, its binding worn, pages ragged; as though it had been asleep for years, woken up just then and decided to fall. My eyes locked on the two words carved into the cover:

Forget Me Not

And another sentence immediately below them, in a tiny script, reminding me I had forgotten everything about that incredible journey of a completely different time and place:

The most mysterious truths are the simplest in the world, since they're the first to be forgotten.

The notebook related a legend. But different from the usual run of legends: this was no tale of heroism. Quite the opposite. It was the tale of a mistake. A short, sparkling tale without a hero that still makes the world nicer and lovelier…

I must recall everything once again. That's why I'm relating all that's written in this notebook today, relating it again. For myself. To recall all that I've long since forgotten.

1

If we have the power to destroy,
does that mean we also have the power to create?

Harsh were the winters in Ida's village, long lay the white blanket of snow on the ground, for months would it lie without lifting. This land far from our sight surrounded by majestic, steep rocks and impassable mountains only showed its face when the sun began to melt the snow, only then did it take a deep breath.

Our story begins on such a day, on a day when sunlight sings of springtime around the corner, glittering on the crystal branches. When Ida was eight, and spring filled her room with the fresh smells of trees and soil… When that mysterious path winked at her from between the lush greens, the path Ida had fantasised about, the path that began where the village ended and wound alongside the stream…

She opened the door of the mud-brick house, silent as a butterfly, too excited to contain herself. She put on her backpack and quietly stepped out. She moved towards the path at the end of the village, her feet sinking into the fast melting snow, soft, melting snow. It was an enchanting view of sunlight reflecting off the snows and the misty crown of the peaks on the horizon. Not that Ida's mind or eyes were in any state to notice the view. Going so far from home on her own for the first time, walking on the path leading to the world beyond the village: could this be the first real taste of freedom? That vast world of freezing cold, wolves howling all night long, mountain fairies,

Aslı Eti

demons, witches petrified by the north winds… all that, and more, an enormous world so long the home of all these ancient tales that somehow rarely mentioned anything nice: all that now lay before her as far as the eye could see. Drunk on freedom, Ida forgot all prohibitions and her whole world changed quite unexpectedly when she pursued a snow tulip.

The mountains soaring all around them were known as glacier peaks. The Heaven and Hell Valley that began where the path ended opened out and deepened towards the horizon. Snowmelt cascaded over vertical boulders and mingled with breaking glaciers to make waterfalls. Icy springs burst forth everywhere. This enchanted place hidden below the misty skies was home to legends older than time itself. As she followed the seemingly endless path, Ida was thinking of the tales of kings, emperors, gods and goddesses, tales that had spread from mouth to mouth. It was as if she were moving into another place and another time as she walked. The misty peaks, clouds and waters raging over sullen, steep rocks all seemed to be transporting her to a land of dreams.

Ida was still on the path when she spotted the snow tulip. It burst into view to the sounds around: the wind, the chirping of the birds and the roaring waterfalls. It just stood there. Silent and harmless… It must have sprouted through the snow. It was the most beautiful thing she had ever seen. Ida had never seen such a tulip, no, such a flower before. Its petals had a velvety white sheen, almost too delicate to touch. They were so tightly wound around one another that the tulip looked like a swan. Dewdrops sparkled on its surface. You couldn't keep your eyes off it once you'd seen it. It was so different from everything around, it looked so different that even though its roots were in the same soil, it could have been brought over from a different universe.

That was nearly the end of the path, and she'd been gone quite a while, her family would soon notice Ida was gone. She had to return to the village as soon as possible. But she couldn't. She just couldn't leave the tulip, just couldn't leave it and go away. Enchanted by the path and intoxicated by the freedom she tasted for the first time, she

Forget Me Not

forgot everything. Just stood and stared at the tulip in the snow. Stared and stared… She had to have it. Absolutely. She couldn't just leave it alone and carry on. She decided to pick it and take it along, to preserve it till the end of time.

She knelt down towards it. Reached out, and just as she was about to pick it, she heard a whisper:

'Don't do it!'

She swung around anxiously, but there was no one around. She reached again and grasped the tulip by the stem. She'd remove it by the roots and replant it once she got back, so it would live in its new home.

'Please don't do it!' repeated the voice.

A little louder this time… A velvety voice, sweet, melodious. Ida looked around again, but there was no one else on the path. She murmured:

'Who's speaking?'

'Me, it's me. Please don't pick me!'

Ida couldn't believe her ears. She stared at the snow tulip in her palm. At its – *her? It sounded like a girl's voice!* - delicate stem, dazzling petals and all around the tree-lined path…

'You,' she said, 'Can you really speak then?'

'Since you can hear me, yes,' replied the tulip.

'I've never seen a speaking flower before… or even heard of one,' said Ida, 'How can you do it?'

'Please let me stay here,' pleaded the tulip. 'I'll die if you pick me.'

'No. I won't kill you. I'll plant you when we get there. Don't worry.'

'No,' said the tulip in a trembling voice. 'I can't live anywhere other than in my own soil, no, oh no! Please don't do it!'

'Why on earth not?' grumbled Ida, 'All flowers live where they're planted; everyone knows that. You're just trying to fool me. Just because you don't want me to pick you…'

'You must believe me; it's the truth,' insisted the tulip. 'I'm special, not like the others.'

'I can tell you're special; you're lovely. That's why I can't just leave you.'

Aslı Eti

'Why ever not?'

'Because I've never had such a lovely thing before. I'll take you home. I'll show you to everyone. No one else has such a beautiful flower; I'll be the only one.'

'But if you pick me, my beauty will fade. I'll just be an ordinary flower if I leave. And I'll fall ill straightaway.'

Ida hesitated. A bit fed up with this whining too: what a carry-on!

'You can't stop me. I'll pick you if I want.'

'You're right... I can't resist you. All I can do is say you shouldn't pick me. You have to believe me.'

'I don't have to believe you. I don't even know you.'

Ida had already decided to pick the snow tulip. She had no intention of chatting any more. She bent down again, grabbed the slender stem nearest the roots and began to pull with all her might. She heard the flower sigh like a cry. Silent dewdrops rolled over the leaves and fell to the ground.

'What a fuss!' said Ida, 'You'll be fine, you won't die, don't worry.'

She carried on pulling with all her strength. She heaved as hard as she could to free it from the soil... Suddenly the snow tulip gave a shrill cry. Freed from the soil's tight hold, the roots burst into view. Ida must have pulled so hard that she reeled back a couple of steps; but she now held the snow tulip.

'There!' she said to herself. She picked up a few twigs and some ivy and made a small basket like her mother had taught her. She filled it with a little soil and buried the roots somewhat untidily. Patting the soil down a little, she admired her work.

'Just like a little flowerpot. Wonderful!'

The snow tulip was crying, whispered pleas unnoticed amongst the sobs.

'Come on, don't be like that,' said Ida, trying to comfort her. 'I'm sorry if I hurt you. Don't worry, I'll look after you really well.'

The tulip's sobs were really annoying. Ida was going to plant her in a pot back home, right? What was the big deal?

4

Forget Me Not

'No matter how well you look after me, it'll be no use,' lamented the tulip. 'It's all over, I can never be the same again…'

Ida turned a deaf ear. All she wanted to do was to go back to her village as soon as possible and show her tulip off to everyone. She'd be the envy of them all! Carrying her flowerpot, she began running towards the start of the path. She ran on the dirt track flanked by a dense row of trees. But the path went on and on. The farther she went, the sparser the woods got. A boulder or two appeared ahead. She looked right, she looked left, she couldn't figure out where the village was. Soon it all looked too unfamiliar. This wasn't anything like the path she'd taken earlier. A valley appeared, growing ever deeper, flanked by steep rocks. There was barely a tree or two; instead, there were weeds and ground lying under snow.

Ida began to feel scared. She looked right, she looked left, looked for someone to ask the way, but there was no one around. She had to leave this valley and turn back towards her village, but she just couldn't find the way no matter what she did or where she looked. Even the path had vanished.

She kept walking, quite hopeless, when a lake appeared, one she'd never seen before. An enormous lake fed by snowmelt. Even framed in mist, it still looked like a huge diamond hanging from its crown of clouds. It was surrounded by wild orchids, pheasant's eyes and scarlet pimpernels.

'Weird!' thought Ida; she'd never heard of such a lake nearby. She took a few steps to take a closer look at the shiny water. She paused to gaze at herself in the water as an inner voice spoke ceaselessly, telling her to get away from this strange place and find her way back as soon as possible. Her absence must have been noticed by now, and her family must be looking for her. But wherever she turned, her way was blocked by boulders or waterfalls big or small. Tired and beginning to feel a little dizzy, she felt a growing unease.

She had no choice but to turn to the snow tulip on her lap.

'I think I'm lost. I have to find my way to the village. Can you help me?'

5

Aslı Eti

'I'm sorry, I can't,' said the tulip, 'I don't know the way.'

In a panic, Ida lost her temper:

'You're just saying that because you're cross with me. To get even. You're from around here, you must know the way.'

'You're wrong; I don't. I've never left my patch before. I've never been this way. Of course I'd tell you if I knew; I want to get back too.'

A dejected Ida sank down onto a boulder and stared at her tulip. The flower looked a little paler compared with a while back, but not enough to worry about. Ida was facing a much bigger problem now: finding her way back as soon as possible. She stood up and began walking in the opposite direction.

'Please take me back to my patch,' said the tulip quietly. 'When you find the path, just plant me back again, will you?'

'No, I won't,' replied Ida, 'Don't you get it? You're mine now. I'm not letting you go.'

'But I don't feel so good; I'm losing my strength. I can't live for long like this. I'll just keep growing weaker. I beg you, please listen...'

'You'll be fine, don't worry,' said Ida, not interested in the tulip's pleas. Her attention was focused on the track ahead, but there was still not a single familiar sight. Backpack on her shoulders, and the tulip in her hands, she wandered on the dirt tracks between those steep rocks for a long while. The track eventually ran out and she found herself in the middle of a seemingly endless meadow. All she could see was the green pasture, clouds, sparrowhawks circling overhead, and in the distance, a haughty mountain, loftier and higher than any she had ever seen before...

She must have been walking for hours; she felt exhausted. She sat down on a boulder for a rest and placed her tulip beside her. That's when she spotted the change in the flower: the head was bowed, staring at the ground instead of the sky. And that bright velvety whiteness had gone too; the petals looked pale, almost muddy. The only sound on the silent pasture was laboured breathing, as if someone was struggling to breathe. That's when it occurred to Ida that the tulip

Forget Me Not

might have been speaking the truth. Feeling uneasy, she bent towards the flower, and asked quietly:

'What's wrong? Are you all right?'

The tulip didn't reply. All that could be heard was the shallow breathing.

'Are you not speaking to me?'

Not a word. No amount of pleading worked; Ida couldn't get a word out. The tulip's silence spoke of despair. She might even stay cross for ever.

Ida looked at the pasture stretching as far as the eye could see, and then lifted her head to stare at the blue skies… An enormous void… There was no sound, not a single sound other than the moaning of the wind gently stroking the grass…

She had no idea which way to go.

Hoisting her backpack and picking up her tulip, she set off again. It was now impossible to figure out where she was heading. She kept walking with no idea what she might meet. There was nothing else she could do. With every step, she heard her own heartbeat and her tulip's breath. Every once in a while, the tulip grew fainter, and even the breathing became inaudible. That's when Ida stopped, scared, listening to her tulip for a few seconds, breathing a sigh of relief only when she heard that faint breath.

A few hours later, an exhausted Ida sank down onto the grass and began to cry quietly:

'I'm sorry. I had no idea…'

Those tears fell on the tulip's petals.

'Please talk, say something, just once. Don't leave me all alone here!'

Ida shed so many tears that the tulip her fill. She seemed to perk up a little; even the breathing improved. Her sobs paused as Ida began listening to the tulip's breathing. The tulip still looked pale grey, but the breathing was much more discernible now.

Trying to gather her strength, the tulip whispered between breaths:

'Look; there's someone over there. Go talk to him.'

Aslı Eti

Ida turned to look, astonished. There was a faint shape ahead, yes, there really was someone there. She was so happy that her tulip had spoken again, and now there was someone to ask directions. Wiping her tears, she pulled herself together.

'I thought you'd stay silent for ever.'

She grabbed her tulip and broke into a stride, talking breathlessly on the way:

'I can do it. I can find my way again. I'm going to go back home…'

And hastened towards the figure ahead.

If you've started, you will finish.
Never stop.

The figure grew larger and came into sharper focus at every step Ida took: it was a shepherd who'd put his sheep out to grass. She grew a little more anxious with each step and slowed down.

'You don't talk to strangers. I hope he's nice.'

The tulip spoke between wheezes:

'Talk to him. He might tell you what you want to know.'

'I will,' replied Ida, 'I don't have a choice. I hope we'll be all right...'

'I have to trust you, and you have to trust him. We don't have a choice,' whispered the tulip.

There were only a few steps between them now. Ida approached slowly. The shepherd was relaxing, stretched out on the grass, his satchel serving as a pillow. He looked only about five or six years older than Ida. He must have noticed her approach, but he was playing it cool. He was watching his flock and keeping rhythm to their bells.

Ida liked hearing the bells, a familiar sound: one she usually heard at home when she got up in the morning. Her fear momentarily forgotten, she smiled, gathered her courage and went over.

'Hello... I... I'm lost, you see... Maybe you can help me.'

The shepherd looked up and greeted her with a nod.

'Where were you going?'

It all poured out: the path, all those tracks, the misty lake, then how she got lost. Everything, except for picking the snow tulip. Quick as a flash, she followed with an impatient question:

'Do you know the way to the village I mean?'

'Course I do,' said the shepherd, still lying down, as cool as a cucumber. He looked like he was enjoying himself. Ida's eyes lit up. The shepherd spoke again just as she was about to ask him to describe the way:

'But first you have to tell me the whole story.'

'I did,' said Ida impatiently.

'No, you didn't,' insisted the shepherd, 'Not everything. That tulip in your hand, for example. Where did you find her?'

Ida bowed her head and looked at her tulip. Just then a dried leaf broke off and fell. It slipped from her fingertips and blew away in the wind before she could do anything about it.

'Never mind; there'd be no point even if you could catch it. It's dead now...'

Ida was left staring after the leaf. Watched it vanish towards the horizon. There was nothing else she could do other than shiver at hearing of the death of a piece of her tulip.

'My tulip's ill. But she will get better.'

'You've wrenched her away from her patch. Shouldn't have.'

His eyes bore into Ida's. He looked as if he expected an explanation.

'How do you know?' asked Ida. Maybe he was bluffing.

'You can tell most things if you look hard,' replied the shepherd. 'You're not telling the truth, because you're only thinking of yourself.'

Ida bit her tongue. She could hear her own heartbeat against the bells.

'You've picked it, right? That is a snow tulip, that is; she can only live in her own soil.'

Ida glanced at her tulip and stroked a few petals as if she were scared to touch them.

'And since she can't really get up and move...' continued the shepherd, 'You must've picked it. It's not rocket science, really.'

Ida bowed her head in shame.

Forget Me Not

'I had no idea…'

'I told you,' said the tulip faintly, sounding like a gentle tune, 'But you wouldn't listen.'

The shepherd nodded. Ida couldn't remember when she'd felt this awful before, no matter how cross she'd made grown-ups. As if she'd committed the greatest crime on earth, and everyone knew about it.

'I thought you were exaggerating,' she bowed her head, her eyes avoiding the tulip… 'Just really wanted you, that's all.'

Neither tulip, nor shepherd spoke. They had both fallen silent. They all stood there for a while. Ida eventually raised her bowed head:

'I'm sorry. I'll make her better; I promise…'

'Not easy,' said the shepherd, patting a lamb on the head. The animal hopped back to its friends. 'That's a very special flower,' the shepherd carried on, 'I'm sure you don't know the prophecy of the snow tulip. Not many do.'

'No…' sighed Ida. She'd never heard of this prophecy.

'All right, listen…' said the shepherd, still lying down. 'Not everyone can see the snow tulip; she's a very rare flower. She's the flower of kindness and beauty. Adorning the world every spring when she re-emerges from the blanket of snow. But she only grows in her own soil. If she's taken out of her patch, everything comes to an end. Both for the picker and the snow tulip. They are both lost then and there. Until…'

He didn't finish. A barely perceptible smile played on his silent lips.

'Until what?' asked Ida impatiently, her heart pounding.

'Until whoever had picked her takes her back. That's the only way they can be reborn. But it's a tough road. Only the picker can go there. And only he or she can make sure to reach the end. No one or nothing else can…'

'What if she doesn't?' she asked, her voice trembling. Terrified at her earlier failure to find her way back to the village.

'Then,' replied the shepherd, still staring at the layers of clouds hanging in the sky, 'She'll have to wander there for ever.'

'And if she does?'

11

Aslı Eti

'Then she will have got there,' laughed the shepherd, 'What more do you want?'

Ida couldn't believe her ears. She felt herself shiver from top to toe. She was hoping the shepherd had made all this up, but something whispered to her that he was telling the truth.

'I must find the way as soon as possible. Since you know about the snow tulip and the prophecy, you must know the way too.'

'Course I do,' replied the shepherd. Still on the ground, he stretched and gazed at Ida's eyes, 'I'll tell you if you do me and my flock a favour.'

'Of course, whatever you want,' said Ida, cheered up at finding someone who knew the way after all these hours. 'What can I do for you?' She thought briefly and took a look around. The only thing she had was her backpack: she opened it, rummaged inside and pulled out a loaf of bread.

'All I have is this loaf; is this any good to you?' she asked, hoping that would make him happy.

'All right,' smiled the shepherd. Ida breathed a sigh of relief. Thankfully she'd found something he might want.

'What're you gonna do when you're hungry though?'

Ida hadn't thought of that. What mattered most was finding her way back as soon as possible.

Saying, 'I'll think about that later; I have to find the way first,' she handed him the loaf.

'OK,' said the shepherd as he took it.

'C'mon then, tell me which way to go?' asked Ida impatiently.

'Beyond that mountain,' replied the shepherd, pointing to the mountain in the distance, the mountain rising to the skies, its peak nearly touching the clouds. Ida stared hopelessly at the lofty mountain higher than all the peaks she knew.

'Are you sure?'

'I'm sure,' laughed the shepherd, 'Everywhere is beyond that mountain.'

Ida was filled with dread. It was impossible to reach that mountain,

Forget Me Not

and even more impossible to climb to the summit even if she did. The shepherd carried on as if he had heard her thoughts:

'It's difficult, but not impossible. Others have done it in the past.'

'Oh, really? Who, for example, and how did they climb so high?' asked Ida curiously. She might pick up a couple of helpful hints.

'I'll tell you if you've got time. They call me the storyteller shepherd around these parts.'

Ida had never heard of a storyteller shepherd before. It sounded like fun. How carefree and jolly he looked!

'I've got time,' she said, sat down next to the shepherd and placed her snow tulip and backpack carefully on the ground. On any ordinary day, she would be rushing here and there, but now it was as if time had stood still. She had all the time in the world anyway. Ever since she was little she'd always loved listening to stories. She remembered the fairy tales her mother told her every night before sleep. Never happy with just the one, she always asked for a second. This thought made her feel totally alone.

'I'll tell you then,' started the shepherd. 'An old man came here once. He had a really long beard and carried a walking stick. He'd obviously been walking for a very long time; he could barely stand as he leant on his stick. He came over, just like you. Caught his breath, told me where he wanted to go and asked me the way. So I told him it lay beyond that mountain.'

'Did he get there?'

'We'll come to that bit later… First he asked me which mountain I meant. That's when I realised he was blind.'

Ida felt sorry for the old man. It must have been hard for a blind man to come all this way… Yet she felt a little brighter. At least she was in a much better condition than that poor fellow. Still, she'd listen to what happened to him first. His advantage was that he wasn't a little girl. She was always told grown-ups could do anything they put their minds and backs to, and children had to wait nicely to grow up. These thoughts were enough to discourage her to give up but she had no other choice. She felt trapped. Then the shepherd spoke, as if once

Aslı Eti

again he'd heard what was on her mind. Could he really do that? How incredible, thought Ida.

'The old man said he felt trapped,' carried on the shepherd, 'Like you. He'd travelled so far that he had no idea where he was. Can you imagine? And he was unable to see that ginormous mountain ahead!'

'What happened next?'

'I described the mountain. Every last detail. I drew an imaginary picture... I told him about every step, every bend, every hillock. And described the way he had to take. That's all I did.'

'Did he manage to find the mountain?'

'At first he was quite dejected. Complained that he was too old to see imaginary pictures. 'Cos' he was just a child last time he'd done that. He was hard work.'

'Then?'

'Then I told him to stop moaning and set off. And he did.'

'So you don't know if he made it or not.'

'Why not? 'Course I do! I know how every story ends. He managed to cross the mountain eventually.'

'But how can you know? You can't have seen him!'

'The birds told me!' laughed the shepherd merrily. 'You do get to hear everything that ever happens sooner or later. So long as you listen carefully...'

Ida hoped he was telling the truth. *Perhaps being a child isn't that bad,* she thought; *it must be much better than getting lost when you're that old...*

'And now you've got to go too,' said the shepherd, making her heart leap into her mouth. Ida stared at the mountain on the horizon.

Still lying on the ground, the storyteller shepherd smiled at her state.

'Big things may not be as big as you think. They just like to look that way,' he said as he reached for the loaf of bread. Ida was puzzled, and surprised the shepherd when she told him she was.

'What don't you get?' he exclaimed, still lying down, 'It's not bigger than the world, is it? No bigger than my hand when you look

Forget Me Not

from here…' He squinted, bent his fingers and grasped the mountain in both hands. Then, with a *Puff!* he opened his hands. He looked like he was having fun.

Ida looked at the green pasture and the cloudy skies. And then at her tulip, silent beside her… It really looked sick. She had to get up and set off soon. To somewhere described by someone she didn't know, towards unknown perils, and with a sick flower… She was on her own for the first time in her life, and would spend the night alone somewhere she didn't know. She could have burst into tears right there, but checked herself. You couldn't cry beside someone you didn't know. She'd been talking to the shepherd all this time, but they were no less distant than that mountain over there. So that's what loneliness meant. Being this far from each other. A few rebellious tears fell.

'You're right,' she said quietly, 'I have to go, I have no other choice. Thanks for showing the way.'

'You're welcome. I'd have done it anyway, even if you hadn't given me your bread.'

'Why?'

She was astonished once again. He was like no one else she knew. He always seemed to say something that surprised her.

'For the tulip's sake, of course! My flock and I will be much happier once she's reunited with her patch.'

'But you're here… so far from my tulip's home. And your flock's with you. Why would you care?'

'Of course we care!' he exclaimed, 'We'll be fine when she's fine. Whenever there is sorrow in some place on Earth, it reaches out and hurts our hearts as well. It's ever been that way.'

'I think you're just putting on airs,' Ida blurted out, 'You're just lying here, enjoying yourself on the grass. And talking of being hurt.' She picked up her tulip and gently stroked the stem.

'Well, here you are,' said the shepherd, even more loudly. 'You're already here. You've upset us, and you're still doing it. Just like I said.'

Ida fumbled for an answer, but nothing came.

Aslı Eti

'To be honest,' carried on the shepherd, 'This is always the way. Now, we'll be delighted if you make us happy before you go.'

'But what can I do?' she asked hopelessly, 'I've given you my bread! I haven't got anything else to give.'

'You're right, that bread will do the job.'

He took a huge bite and began to chew hungrily:

'Yummy! You don't always find such good bread here,' he murmured, chewing noisily. He ate with such appetite that Ida felt a little hungry herself. What she wouldn't give for a bite... She swallowed, licked her lips, but didn't say a word. Just watched him. He swallowed his mouthful and flung the rest of the load to the edge of the puddle a little way away.

'Why did you throw it?' asked Ida. 'That was all I had to eat! You should have given me the rest if you weren't going to eat it.'

'But it's ours; you gave it to us,' replied the shepherd calmly, 'And that means we can do what we like with it. And what I'm gonna do is give the birds a proper feast.'

'But there are no birds around!' insisted Ida. She couldn't remember when she'd been this angry over a mouthful of bread. So you really could fight someone for a bite of bread...

'Don't be cross. They'll come. They come every evening when we have food. It's quiet around here at night. So the birds cheer us up when they come. We'll enjoy a feast and a jolly evening with our chirping friends, and we'll be happy. We'll remember you and send you our thanks.'

He smiled. His flock perked up at his words, and the bells sounded a lot louder. 'You'd better go now,' his voice rose amongst the bells.

'I'd better go now,' said Ida, 'Better find my way before dark. Maybe you can come with us for a while and show the way?'

'Impossible,' replied the shepherd, 'Like I said: only you can go that way. I can't leave this place anyway; my flock couldn't cope with the journey. You must go on your own.'

Ida hoisted her backpack, cradled her tulip and forced a smile:

'Good bye, then.'

Forget Me Not

The shepherd nodded back, calling out, 'Good luck!' behind her departing back.

As Ida and the tulip set off, the pasture broke out into birdsong. Evening was falling, and the storyteller shepherd must have been feeling happy enough to play a sweet tune on his pipe.

'A happy home,' sighed the tulip, 'You wouldn't be scared if you'd stayed there. Wouldn't be alone either.'

'Yes, but it's not my home. I'm going back to my home.'

The flock's bells and the birdsong grew fainter, stayed back on the pasture well behind them now… And eventually were heard no more.

3

Listen carefully, and you might hear a tree whisper. And so much more...

Ida walked on until the pasture was left far behind, her gaze focused on the mountain ahead. She wanted to get there in a jiffy, but no matter how far she walked, she seemed to be standing on the spot. It still looked too far.

'It's impossible to reach it tonight,' she told her tulip. Worryingly for the tulip, Ida was panting and slowing down, barely able to stand. They were still only at the start; at this rate, they would never reach the base of the mountain. The tulip had to do something before it was too late. Gathering her strength, she asked, 'That backpack of yours; what's in it?'

'My things,' said Ida grumpily, too tired to chat after that long trek.

'It looks heavy. Why don't you drop it?'

'Never!' exclaimed Ida, 'I'd have nothing left if I did.'

'Do you need them though?'

'Of course! I need them all. Maybe not now, but later.'

'But it's slowing you down,' came the anxious reply. Unless they were very careful, they might never reach their destination, no matter how much they avoided mentioning that prospect.

'Soon you'll be totally exhausted. At this rate we'll never reach my patch,' the tulip blurted out, concerned at the prospect of perishing in the middle of this strange place.

Forget Me Not

Ida paused and glanced at the tulip, barely holding back the tears.

'All you think about is yourself. All you care about is getting back to your soil. You never think about me.'

She was at the end of her tether. The farthest this little girl had ever gone on her own before was the road behind her home. She couldn't possibly survive this journey.

'Maybe I should never have tried to take you back!' came out before she could stop herself.

'Drop me if you like,' said the tulip, that velvety voice on the verge of tears. 'I can't stop you.'

'I can't, though! You'd die if you were left on your own here.'

She remembered the shepherd's words: she could only go back if she returned the tulip to her patch first. And he'd also said they were always upset by wrongdoing, no matter where it came from. He could be right. And what was the point of leaving the tulip, anyway? Other than leaving Ida all on her in these strange lands.

'I won't leave you,' she said, 'I can manage.'

'Can you show me what's in the backpack?'

'OK.'

Ida placed the flowerpot on the ground carefully, opened the backpack and emptied it: a small kite, a ragdoll, a wooden figure of a horse, a blanket, a bottle of water, pencil and paper, a few walnuts, and pebbles she'd gathered in the rear garden at home…

'And I had a loaf of bread too, but gave it to the shepherd.'

'So many things!' said the tulip, astonished. 'Do you really need them all?'

'That's nothing. I have lots more where I come from.'

'Really?'

The tulip was puzzled: what could you do with so much stuff? But Ida spoke so naturally that it must be normal where she came from.

'I couldn't go a single day without them. Don't you have anything of yours?'

'Of course I do. Nothing that I have to carry though. The sky gives me all I need. And it's found everywhere.'

19

'What, for example?'

'A little soil, a little water, sunlight, fresh air, butterflies and bees... That's all. I couldn't go a single day without them.'

'You're lucky,' murmured Ida.

'But you've got them all too, don't you?'

'Actually, I do.'

'Perhaps you don't need anything else either,' said the tulip innocently. She was like no one or nothing Ida knew. She might not be as lovely as she was when she'd first spotted it, but she was good company.

'We need much more in the world of humans,' replied Ida. She was packing her bag again. 'Grown-ups work day and night for more; they say we can't live otherwise. They're so scared of being left with nothing. That's why all they do is work. Otherwise they'd be paupers, and no one helps paupers.'

'How awful! Maybe they just think so?'

'Maybe. But grown-ups say they know everything.'

'Do they know about me as well then?'

'You? They know the legend, of course. But I don't think they really know you because they've never seen you.'

'So they don't know everything,' mused the tulip, sounding very serious. 'There must be other things they don't know.'

'Maybe. They certainly don't know you can speak. No one would ever believe it.'

'Yes I can, and can speak to them too.'

'You don't get it... They wouldn't believe it even if you did. They'd think they were going crazy; they'd pop pills, they'd be scared, and they'd think they were dreaming, so they wouldn't tell anyone. They'd run to a doctor in secret... So you're right, we can't say they know everything.'

'You believe me, though...'

'Why wouldn't I? Here you are, with me.'

Ida had packed up and it was time to get a move on. 'It'll be dark soon,' she said, shivering. The sun was starting to descend on the

Forget Me Not

horizon, painting the sky golden yellow. She looked up at the mountain in the distance again… She'd never seen such a high mountain in all her life. Trees had begun to appear on the way as she walked. Tall trees, growing ever thicker. The sky darkened. It was pitch black. They couldn't see anything.

'I'm scared,' said Ida.

'Don't be. There's nothing to be scared of. It's just a forest. Let's find somewhere to spend the night.'

'I don't like the dark,' said Ida, nailed to the spot, her words nearly drowned by sobs.

'Look,' said the tulip, trying to be heard, 'There's a huge tree over there, where we can spend the night. And the stars will shine soon, don't worry.'

Whispers rose from everywhere in the forest. Ida shut her eyes tight. She wished it would all come to an end, she wished to find herself back in her room when she opened her eyes. Too tired to take even one more step, she just stood there for a few minutes. But you couldn't spend the whole night standing still. And she was tired, and beginning to feel cold too.

'Please,' whispered the tulip, 'The tree is just there. Just a few steps…'

Trying to gather her courage, Ida took a couple of steps towards the tree. They felt like the most difficult steps she'd ever taken. She'd never been so alone last time she was scared. As she hugged the flowerpot, she felt her palms sweat.

The tulip began to pant, as if she were choking, but bravely kept silent. Her leaves were touching Ida's hands that enfolded her. She'd have encouraged Ida a little bit if she weren't that weary. All she could do was plead with Ida to take a few more steps.

Ida's sobs grew fainter, more sighs now. She made it to the tree, hugged it as if grasping a lifebelt, caught her breath and felt a little better.

'Look! The stars are starting to twinkle,' said the tulip, 'Such a cheerful sight! I always loved it, ever since I was little.'

Ida looked up to the sky. A couple of stars winked at her. The tulip tried to cheer Ida up, but it didn't seem to be working:

'When the stars twinkle, that means it's nearly time to go to sleep.'

'I've never slept outdoors before. And I'm hungry besides. I can't go to sleep on an empty stomach.'

She gave in to a new bout of sobbing. As she cried, she rummaged in her backpack. She picked up one of the walnuts, popped it into her mouth and chewed and chewed. Just as she was about to eat the second, she paused, changed her mind and placed it back in her bag. She didn't know how long the journey would take. She might need the remaining walnuts later.

'I'm hungry too,' said the tulip, sounding a bit wheezy again, 'Could you water my pot please?'

'Sorry, I'd forgotten,' said Ida. She poured a little water into the pot from her bottle. The tulip drank it all.

'Thank you, that's great.'

Ida swallowed a few drops carefully, making sure not to spill a single one. She took her blanket out of the backpack, drew it over herself and leant against the tree. All she wanted to do was to close her eyes and not open them till the morning.

'My family must be looking for me. They must be out of their minds with worry,' she said, 'Should we try to shout? Maybe they'll hear us.'

'I don't think I could manage it; I can barely stand upright anyway. Blow and I'll fall. You go ahead if you want.'

That's when a whisper broke the silence. Ida's heart leapt into her mouth; she was frozen to the spot and her heart was pounding.

'Don't bother; they can't find you here.'

'Did you hear it too?' Ida whispered, without moving a muscle. 'I did.'

'What was that voice? Where did it come from?'

The same voice whispered again:

'Don't be scared; there's nothing to be scared of. It's just me.'

'Who are you?' asked Ida, her eyes shut tight.

'Me. You're leaning on me now.'

Ida leapt to her feet and flung herself away; scared, all she could do was stare at the tree rising in front of her.

'You? You mean... This voice comes from the tree?'

'Yes,' joined the tulip, not in the least bit bothered. As if all this was perfectly normal. 'That's where the voice is coming from.'

The same voice spoke again. It wasn't scary at all, in fact; if anything, it sounded almost familiar:

'They can't possibly find you here. Or rather, they can't possibly find this place.'

'Why?' asked Ida, 'Where are we? Why do you say that?'

'Well, we're in the forest, of course... But they can't come here. In the past, maybe, but now...' The tree paused; a deep sigh, then the leaves seemed to shiver. 'Now it's impossible, believe me...'

Ida took a couple of steps towards the tree and knelt down under it.

'If you know this, then you must know how I can find them. Please tell me. I'll give you whatever you want. I mean, I'll try...'

The tree chuckled.

'I don't want anything from you. But I can give you something else. Even if I cannot answer your question. Because I don't know the answer.'

'Why is it that everyone only knows *some* things?' Ida mumbled.

'Come closer,' said the tree, 'Look up. See the plums on my branches. Eat your fill... You look exhausted. My leaves are soft; make a pillow.'

Ida came closer. 'I can't say no to plums!'

She climbed up in a trice, settled on a branch and fell upon the plums. She gorged herself so much that her stomach swelled; it was huge now.

The tree chuckled again.

'You came just at the right time then. You must have been starving!'

'The strangest supper I've ever had. But it was delicious, thank you.'

'You're welcome.' A faint breeze rose from somewhere. Ida had an

23

Aslı Eti

odd feeling, as if the leaves were stroking her hair. She stared at the tree, at the trunk, branches and leaves...

'You're staring as if you were seeing me for the first time,' said the tree cheerfully.

'I am. I mean, I've seen lots of trees before, but not you.'

Humming a soft tune, the tree said, 'Look up. The stars are twinkling. Don't miss it.'

'My tulip had said the same thing!' said Ida, surprised. She looked up. A couple of stars twinkled. Then ten, then a hundred, then a thousand... The sky was a sea of light now. Never having seen the sky like this before, Ida was mesmerised. Her gaze then travelled down the branches reaching out to the sky, travelled down the branches to the trunk, and then to the earth beneath. Starlight reflected on the leaves. It was a wonderful sight.

'I hadn't noticed how lovely you were!'

'Go to sleep now,' said the tree, 'You've got a long way to go tomorrow.'

'How do you know?' asked Ida, climbing down.

'Since you're here at this late hour, you must be a wayfarer; ergo, you have somewhere to go. It's not that hard to figure out.'

'You're right,' said Ida with a yawn; her body felt very heavy after such an exhausting day. Resting her back against the tree, she carefully placed her tulip beside her. With a 'Good night!' to the tulip, she drew the blanket over herself. No longer hungry, and a little more relaxed, Ida was still scared: it was the first time she would ever sleep on her own in the forest. On her own, if, that is, you didn't count the tulip or the tree...

'Don't worry,' whispered the tree, 'I'll stay awake all night and keep an eye on you.'

Ida felt the same faint breeze on her neck again, a strange feeling as if someone were stroking her hair... She was too tired to think.

'I don't know how to thank you.'

That soft chuckle floated in the air once again:

'Just don't forget tonight!'

Forget Me Not

The rising moon illuminated the forest. Ida, the tulip and the tree were left alone with the moon and the stars.

And Ida fell into a deep sleep as soon as she closed her eyes.

4

The earth is your home.
You can't live cooped up in some corner.

They woke up at dawn. What actually woke Ida up was the wheezing of her tulip though. She dribbled a little water into the pot. The tulip breathed a little easier. It must have lost a few more petals in the night; she looked quite weak and feeble now. That graceful neck seemed to be bent towards the ground. Most of her petals were gone. Ida's heart sank. What a terrible feeling this was, this helplessness! She was too young to look after someone else... She remembered how she drove everyone up the wall whenever she fell ill. But her tulip didn't complain at all; she never asked for anything unless she was in real trouble.

'Are you cold?' Ida asked tentatively.

'A little,' replied the tulip, 'I can manage. At least for the time being...'

'We'd better get a move on,' said Ida, ate a couple of plums and packed a few for later. Repeating her thanks, she took her leave of the tree, cradled her tulip, and set off towards the mountain. The forest didn't look in the least bit intimidating in daylight.

'What a lovely welcome it was!' said the tulip, 'What a nice tree! Making us feel at home.'

'Yes,' agreed Ida, 'It was a fine home, the tree. But not our home. We still have a long way to go.'

Forget Me Not

They proceeded for quite a while without a break. Ida was all right at first, but she grew increasingly tired; whenever she tried to pick up speed, she started huffing and puffing. She was aching all over. She wasn't used to walking non-stop like this. She considered discarding a few of her belongings to lighten her backpack, but dropped the idea straightaway. They stopped for a few drops of water every so often. But their water stock was diminishing; they had to find water somewhere in the forest. What was left in the bottle would only see them through for one more day, if that. Ida grew more and more tired. She thought everything must seem more achievable in the morning, and more impossible at sunset. Or perhaps it just seemed that way to her... She must have made it up: the road was the same morning and night. What did they have to do with the road? And anyway, lots of different thoughts passed through her mind; she was obviously unable to think clearly. She felt brave one moment, and scared the next; strong one moment, and the weakest thing in the world the next. Confused, unable to tell which feeling to trust. All she knew was that the idea of never going back home filled her with the greatest dread. What she didn't care about was whether she was brave or cowardly: all she wanted was to be back home.

After a few more hours on the road, the trees seemed to draw back on either side to give way: a lush green plain opened up before to Ida and her tulip, and the mountain on the horizon seemed a little closer. All the same, Ida couldn't be sure. It might be closer, but then again, it might not...

'Let's take a rest here,' she said, 'I can't go on if we don't.'

She found a tree to lean against; just as she was about to sit down, she heard a totally unexpected noise in the distance. Like an accordion? Playing the nicest tune she'd ever heard. An emotional and touching melody...

'Did you hear that?' she asked her tulip, astonished.

'Yes,' replied the tulip.

'Sounds like an accordion... But how do you get music in the middle of the forest? Is there a village or a town nearby? Are we saved?'

Aslı Eti

'I don't know. Listen: it's getting closer.'

'Yes.'

Ida was nailed to the spot, clutching her tulip. She was scared, but equally curious about the source of the music. The more she listened, the more enchanting it sounded, nice enough to cheer her up.

As the sound came closer, a young boy appeared ahead, playing the accordion, and walking towards them. Wearing a felt hat with a single feather tucked into the band, and a shirt of many colours, he could have leapt out of a fairy tale. Another person in this strange forest! And a child at that… He looked about the same age as Ida, who was awestruck, yet impatient to talk to him. Maybe he was going to the village; if so, he could show them the way.

He, too, had spotted Ida by now, and waved as he approached.

'Hi!'

'Hi,' said Ida with a cautious smile, still sitting.

'My name is Jal,' said the boy, extending his hand.

'And mine's Ida.'

They shook hands. It felt strange, this seemingly routine introduction in the middle of the forest. The boy looked in fine spirits; he looked happy. Not at all as if he might be lost or scared.

'What're you doing here?' asked Jal.

'I'm lost. I'm looking for the way back home. Why are you here; are you lost too?'

'Noo,' replied Jal, 'I'm just taking a stroll. It's a nice day.'

'You mean you live here?' asked an astonished Ida, 'Your home, family: all here?'

'Yes. I mean, for the time being,' said Jal, 'I'll introduce you if you like.'

Ida didn't reply straightaway. She hesitated. It all sounded a little confusing. Surely Jal and his family couldn't be living in the depths of the forest? That's when the tulip piped up:

'He looks nice; let's go meet them.'

'Hey!' exclaimed Jal, eyes wide open in surprise, 'Your flower can speak!'

Forget Me Not

'Yes,' smiled Ida, 'You may greet my tulip.'

Jal immediately assumed a grave air. Bowing like a noble prince, he extended his arms in a formal greeting:

'How do you do, dear tulip; you look lovely today!'

With a velvety laugh, a bashful tulip thanked the boy.

'Looks like she hasn't received much in the way of compliments of late. Shame... A flower needs constant flatter. You, too, look lovely, Ida!'

His greeting ended with a brief tune on his accordion; he was, actually, quite good.

'A talking flower. What a lucky day. Fifika's going to love it!'

'Who's Fifika?' asked Ida, never having heard this name.

'You'll see soon,' said Jal, 'You're coming with me, right?'

'All right,' said Ida, and they set off. *Such a fun fellow!* Making them laugh in spite of everything. What's more, he wasn't in the least bit fazed by a talking tulip; instead he was pleased. *He's incredible,* thought Ida.

'It's not far; our home's just beyond that copse.' They were both striding now. Jal began playing his accordion again. This time it was a different tune, lively and cheerful. The trees and bushes all looked much nicer with this melody in the background. How was it possible that this huge forest could look so different in just a couple of minutes?

A thickly wooded patch led to a narrow path. Ida couldn't believe her eyes at the sight of the small, flat heath a little ahead. Several horse carriages stood to one side: two-wheel caravans, with thick fabric stretched between the poles on all four corners. In the middle of the heath was a burst of colour: people wandering amongst wooden tables and chairs. They were talking in such loud voices, and laughing so heartily... that it looked like a festival. Ida was nailed to the spot in astonishment.

'There!' exclaimed Jal proudly, 'My family.'

'What a big family! But you'd said your home was around here too?'

Aslı Eti

'And so it is,' said Jal, pointing to one of the caravans. 'We carry our homes with us,' he laughed.

Ida was confused. How do you carry your home with you? Everyone had one home and that was that. Simple. Tickled at that pensive look, Jal grabbed her by the hand and hurried downhill, towards the heath.

'Us gipsies are wanderers. It's a matter of pride with us.'

'I had no idea...' said Ida.

'And we never leave our homes behind. So we can live wherever we want.'

Ida had never heard anything like this before; *What a nice custom!* she thought.

Once on the heath, they wandered amongst the crowd in colourful outfits. The men all wore hats and broad braces holding up their trousers. All the women were extravagantly dressed in long, frilly skirts, and wore make-up and flowers in their hair. And everyone was barefoot. Rushing this way and that, some setting out the tables and chairs as others hung colourful lanterns on the trees. Women surrounding the huge cauldron boiling over the fire ahead were singing and keeping rhythm. There were pigeons everywhere, alighting on shoulders, hats and tables. Jal greeted everyone he passed, and they all greeted him back. Some even nodded a greeting to Ida and said something with a smile, but in an unfamiliar language. They trotted on until they suddenly halted facing an ancient woman sitting cross-legged under a tree. Extremely long, pure white hair framed a deeply wrinkled face; she must have been at least a hundred. Maybe even older. With a loud kiss on her cheek, Jal said something in that unfamiliar tongue. The old woman looked Ida from top to toe, nodded a greeting and gestured her to sit down.

A tense Ida looked at Jal, as if unsure what to do. 'Go on. Sit down,' he laughed, 'This is my grandma. Patia.'

'Hello,' said Ida tentatively. 'Does she understand me?'

Jal laughed out loud once again:

Forget Me Not

'Of course she does! She understands everything. I told her you were lost. She might be able to help you. She can see the future, see.'

'You're kidding, right?' asked Ida, 'No one can see the future!'

'Says who?' retorted Jal, 'That's what you think. Patia can, and how. She's never been wrong.'

'Oh...' said Ida, staring at Patia wordlessly as if spellbound. Jal said something to Patia in that language again. Whatever it was, it made her chuckle. She reached out and stroked Ida's hair.

'Ida,' she began and moved to her tongue. She had a deep voice.

'She says not to trust your eyes much,' said Jal. He was seated next to Ida, cross-legged, as he interpreted Patia's words.

'What's that supposed to mean?' asked Ida, 'I don't get it...'

'She says there's much more than you can see around you...'

Patia said something else and pointed to the tulip. Ida handed over her flowerpot carefully. You couldn't say no to Patia; there was something strange in her gaze, something that made you feel you had to obey.

Patia took the pot, bent over the tulip and whispered something. Suddenly the tulip stopped wheezing quite so much. Patia returned the pot, but she was frowning. The index finger wagging in the air suggested that whatever she was saying, it wasn't nice.

'You should never have picked it,' said Jal, 'Patia says you should never take a decision on someone else's behalf. It was totally wrong. Every child should have his or her own story.'

'All right,' replied Ida, blushing bright red. She explained she was taking her tulip back to her patch. And she had to get home as soon as possible too. Perhaps Patia could help her? Since she could see the future, maybe she could tell her what to do, how to get back?

'Not now, she says,' said Jal, 'She's going to have her beauty nap and she's really cross with you for what you did to the flower. Maybe later, she says.'

Ida was reluctant to miss the chance of help from someone who could see the future, now that she'd found someone like that. And it really wasn't realistic for a hundred-year-old to want a beauty nap.

31

Aslı Eti

'Beauty nap? Are you serious?' she asked Jal.

"Course I'm serious,' replied Jal, 'Tell Patia yourself if you like, that you don't take her beauty nap seriously.' His face broke into a cheeky grin.

'OK, OK, shut up. Don't let her hear you. I won't say a thing!' she whispered, hoping Patia hadn't understood. She didn't dare look at the grandmother as she spoke. With a despondent move, she took her leave and followed Jal to the middle where the tables stood. They'd walked a fair bit when she asked impatiently:

'She'll read my future later though, right?'

'Don't know; she might. If you don't annoy her, that is.'

They kept wandering in the heath; the hustle and bustle around them only seemed to have increased. Colourful lanterns now hung from the trees and there was feverish activity around the tables.

'What're they all doing? What's all the rush?' asked Ida.

'They're getting ready,' replied Jal, his face brightening. 'Today's a great day. We have a wedding this evening!' He looked very happy.

'Really? Who's getting married?'

'Fifika, my big sister I mean. She's marrying Tobar. He's a great poet and bird trainer.'

He sounded very proud as he spoke of Tobar: so these had to be prestigious professions for him and his family then.

'And I'm his apprentice. One day I'll be a great poet like him. Except I've yet to find a single rhyming couplet. That's why Tobar says I'm more likely to become a musician.'

As she laughed, Ida momentarily forgot she was all on her own in the middle of some strange forest. Jal's world was too colourful to resist.

'What a lovely world you have!' said the tulip before taking a few deep breaths.

'Yes, we do,' said Jal, 'But I think all worlds are lovely.'

'Mine is lovely too,' sighed the tulip, 'I hope you can come and see it one day. I have to get back first, of course…'

'Of course,' said Jal, 'I'd be delighted to visit.'

Forget Me Not

Ida thought about the tulip's world, and Jal's, and the storyteller shepherd's and the tree's. And her own... So you could have lots of different worlds all at the same time in this world... Her own home was lovely too. But she couldn't invite Jal to stay. Her parents would never think it safe to invite a traveller child. And if they ever saw Patia, they would surely have a fit. They would never let Ida go anywhere near Patia once they calmed down. *Sometimes grown-ups really don't understand a thing,* thought Ida.

A clutch of young girls fluttered a little way ahead.

'What are they doing?' asked Ida.

'They're dressing the bride up. That's where Fifika is, look,' he said, and broke into a run, yelling, 'Fifikaaa!' He broke into the circle, and Ida followed with her tulip. Fifika was sitting on a stool in the middle, her long black hair adorned with flowers and wearing a long dress of colourful gauze, long enough to reach the ground. It bared her shoulders and arms. Her skin was very pale and her lips were painted bright red. There was a pigeon on her hand. She was so beautiful that she looked like a fairy. She smiled when she spotted Jal, and stroked his head. The girls broke into a new song as they painted motifs on their arms in some dark dye. One grasped Ida's hand to draw a picture: a moon and sun looking at each other. Ida loved it.

The wedding party began at sunset. Apparently all parties begin when the moon and the sun are in the sky at the same time. Ida asked Jal why. He replied, "Cos' that's the moment when seemingly the most impossible things get together, when everything is possible. It's magic. It brings happiness.' Ida looked at the drawing on her hand; it had to mean something then... She grasped the drawing with her other hand and dreamt of hugging her mother again.

There was an enormous feast table in the middle of the heath. Everyone sat down. Patia sat at the head of the table; Fifika and Tobar sat on either side of her. Jal and Ida found seats side by side.

'That's the greatest feast table in the world!' exclaimed Jal, 'My belly's rumbling, I'm so hungry.'

Ida was starving too; she'd had no hot food for over a day. She

33

Aslı Eti

was so hungry, she felt she couldn't wait another minute. The first course was a delicious hot soup. Then something else came, some indescribably yummy dishes wrapped in leaves that Ida didn't recognise.

Ida and Jal polished off their plates in a flash, Ida watered her tulip generously and drank a few glasses herself. Some of the wedding party stood up, now that they'd eaten, and picking up their violins, began to play. The sun had set and the stars were beginning to twinkle in the sky. Conversation and laughter rang around the table for a while longer.

Then the table was cleared. The wedding party gathered around the big fire. In the stillness since the violins had fallen silent, everyone settled down around the fire, and Ida and Jal followed suit.

'Now what?' whispered Ida into Jal's ear, taking care not to break the silence.

'Poems,' replies Jal, 'This is the custom. Tobar will first offer his love to the trees, birds and the sky. Then to our family. And finally to Fifika.'

'Really? How romantic!'

'It is. Others will join in too. They, too, will speak. In the end it all becomes one single poem. This is very important.'

'Why?' asked Ida inquisitively. She'd never heard of such a custom before, and it sounded really nice.

'Because we love everything all at once, not separately. It has to be a single poem that everyone joins in.'

'Wonderful! A single poem that loves everything.'

'The more crowded the poem, the nicer it is,' Jal continued. 'I mean, the more people join the better it is. Love will be that big then. Simple really.'

'Yes, actually...' pondered Ida, 'I'll tell them when I get back.'

Just then two more people came and sat down around the fire.

'That's why it's important that none of us is missing around the fire,' explained Jal, 'We wait for everyone to come and sit down.

Forget Me Not

Tonight, for example, you're an extra, we're even more crowded, which is great.'

'Am I going to recite a poem too?' asked Ida in a panic.

'Of course you are! You wouldn't want to risk Patia's fury now, would you?' laughed Jal.

'Never!' said Ida and fell silent. Her heart was pounding.

'Keep calm,' said the tulip on her lap, 'I'm sure you'll do fine.' It was close enough to her heart to feel the pounding in her own body.

Everyone was seated now, except for Tobar, who was standing up by the fire. Fifika sat facing him. The rest of the party had formed a circle a few steps away from the fire. Patia sat at the head of the front row. The heath in the middle of the forest was utterly still. No one made a sound. All that could be heard was the crackling of the branches feeding the fire. The sky was thick with stars. The moon hung like an enormous lantern in the middle of the sky. Then a soft flute rose up. One of the young men had walked up to the fire and begun to play an emotional melody as time seemed to stand still.

Tobar took a deep breath and started reciting his first poem, of his love for the trees, birds and the sky... As the words flowed, Jal interpreted for Ida's benefit, pointing out he didn't always manage to get the rhyme:

Every stone on my path
Shares a secret with me
Every breath I draw
From the bluest sky
To the darkest sea
Is a blessing for me

Everyone cheered. The flute continued playing its spellbinding tune.

Another poet stood up after Tobar to share his words with the wedding party:

If I was a cloud in the sky
Or a wave in the sea
If I was a handful of earth

Aslı Eti

Or a single raindrop
I would still be a huge world
With skies and stars and oceans inside me

Others took their turn one by one. The party cheered every poet. Next, it was time for Tobar to offer his love to the family. He started quietly, sounding a little melancholy, gazing at the flames. Jal carried on translating. Ida noticed his voice trembled near the end.

Time has wings,
So do people.
They both fly away
Freely.
I never forget...
Nothing ever vanishes;
Everything
Comes back to join me

Jal turned away before finishing his translation. Ida could feel his silent sobs. Wanting to spare his blushes, she sat wordlessly.

It was someone else's turn to recite. Then another's, and another's. Ida waited for Jal to stop crying and turn back. That's when she felt she could bring herself to ask what Tobar's poem meant. Jal was much calmer now, and he translated the nicest words Ida had ever heard.

'It speaks of family members who've passed on; Tobar sent them his love. My parents included.'

He avoided her gaze as he spoke, staring instead into the distance. Ida felt herself welling up; she had no idea he lived with such a great loss. She was about to say something, but changed her mind. So he was all on his own in this world – never mind the huge, colourful crowd. She thought children who weren't alone were more fortunate than those who were.

It took a while, but Jal finally opened up. His parents had died in a fire when he was very young. It was the middle of the might when a fire broke out in their caravan, when everyone was in deep sleep. The flames had woken up everyone, and people ran away, but it was too late for some. Jal's parents must have been surrounded by the flames

Forget Me Not

when they woke up. The tribe had rushed to the rescue, sure, risking their own lives, but no one had been able to do anything. Jal and Fifika happened to be staying with Patia in her caravan nearby that night, which is how they had survived.

'Afterwards, we left that camp and moved over here,' said Jal, 'To our new home. Sometimes I get the feeling they might have accompanied us...'

The lump in her throat prevented Ida from offering solace even though she really wanted to comfort him; except, she didn't know what to say.

One thing she was sure of was that words could never put out the fire Jal would never forget.

Several of the party recited something, and eventually it was Ida's turn. Her heart was pounding, but her tulip gave her courage with a whispered, 'Don't worry, just tell them what you feel...'

Ida hesitated in silence, not knowing what to say. She could profess her love for her own family as a visitor. Her heart felt like it would stop, she felt she was choking. With a gaze at her hands interlaced on her lap, she blurted out the words inside:

No matter how far apart we are
We will hug again
Just like the moon and the star.

Everyone cheered her poem. Ida was astonished, especially as she'd never recited a poem before. In fact, she had never even spoken before such a large gathering before! She was delighted at having given a good account of herself, but she really missed home! That longing overshadowed the pleasure. Jal tried to cheer her up:

'Why did you hide you were a great poet?' he exclaimed, 'I'd have asked for lessons if I knew!'

Ida forced a smile, before noticing Patia's stare and taking her gaze away.

It was the final part of the ceremony. It was now time for Tobar to profess his love for Fifika, and then they would plight their troth.

Aslı Eti

Fifika stood up and came up to Tobar. They held hands. Tobar looked her in the eye and recited:

The greatest magic
In all the world
Is entering your heart
From far away
Without even touching your hand.

There was wild cheering. Jal yelled, 'I told you he was a great poet, didn't I?' He leapt up to join in the applause.

Tobar and Fifika promised each other their eternal love and protection. And they were married. Renewed laughter broke the silence; the flute was joined by violins and accordions. Dancing broke out around the fire. Ida danced with Jal for a while; she hadn't had this much fun in a long time.

The party went on for a long time as some danced to the music, and others simply milled around the fire. Fifika and Tobar had stopped dancing; they were now chatting to their friends. Jal dragged Ida by the sleeve over to the newlyweds for congratulations. That's when Fifika spotted the tulip Ida was carrying.

'What's that you're holding? It's a tulip of sorts, but looks quite different,' she said.

'This is a snow tulip, like in the famous legend… She's very rare. She's a bit poorly now. That's why she looks so feeble and pale grey. I'm taking her back to make her better.'

Jal blurted out, 'Fifika, did you know that this flower can speak?'

'Oh, really?' asked Fifika, excited. She asked Ida, 'May I chat to her?'

'All right,' said a reluctant Ida. It would be rude to refuse a bride at her wedding.

Fifika took the little pot and spoke to the tulip:

'Hello.'

The tulip's 'Hello,' in that lovely, soft voice clearly impressed Fifika.

Forget Me Not

'Can I have her as a wedding present?' she asked Ida, 'I'll give you one of Patia's best, most special tulips.'

She ran to fetch one of Patia's famous tulips and came back with an enormous, breathtakingly lovely pink specimen with gleaming velvety petals. Its heady scent filled the air. All eyes were fixed on the tulip now... No one looked at anything else. No one heard Ida's tulip's breath quickening - except for Ida, that is.

'How about it? Would you give me your flower as a gift? Patia's tulips are extraordinary. They are the most beautiful tulips in the world, totally unique.'

The pink tulip's beauty could not be expressed in words, true. Ida paused for a look at the flower.

'Yes, Patia's tulip is really spellbinding,' she agreed, 'Difficult to refuse... But the tulip you're holding is no ordinary flower. That is my friend. You'd never give your friend away, would you?'

Fifika hesitated at first... Then, with a sulky, 'Suit yourself!' she handed the pot back and resumed chatting with her friends. Ida hugged her tulip's pot, brought her ear closer and listened carefully: the tulip's breathing was calmer, less wheezy. She felt a bit better.

Ida had surprised herself with her words. But they were true... She and the tulip were each other's only friends. She'd hardly given the tulip a thought up to now as all she was concerned with was finding her way back home. To be honest, her tulip was no longer the breathtaking beauty she'd first spotted. It looked no different from all the other flowers around. If anything, she looked even weaker and paler than most. All the same, Ida couldn't even imagine carrying on without her. Yes, she had to return her to her patch before she could go back, but she had no idea if she'd ever succeed. And even if she didn't need to, she didn't want to even think of being all alone here, in these strange lands, without her tulip. All this made them friends of a sort. But could you become friends with someone who'd caused your present troubles? Perhaps her tulip didn't see her as a friend after all this, and never would. And she'd be totally justified. Ida couldn't be

39

Aslı Eti

selfish enough to demand friendship, could she? There was nothing to say. Still, she felt better for having refused to part with her tulip.

The party was drawing to a close, and she was watching the dancers in the middle with Jal, when Ida felt a hand on her shoulder. Swinging around brought her face to face with Patia, who said something in her language, and gestured Ida to follow. They sat down in a nook a little way from the crowd, facing one another. Patia took Ida's hand, turned the palm up to the sky, gazed for a few seconds and began to speak. Jal was translating:

'She says the prophecy's come true. But don't lose heart; the stars are with you. Your palms are filled with stars. This means you're kind-hearted, and will attain your goal.'

Ida was thrilled, and equally terrified: so the prophecy the shepherd had mentioned was real!

'Will I go back home, you mean?' she asked impatiently, fixing her wide eyes on Jal.

'You will reach your goal at journey's end, but your journey won't be over,' said Jal after listening to Patia.

'What do you mean? I don't get it…'

'That's what she said. She said one more thing: one drop can give birth to a forest. Never forget it.'

Patia stood up and moved towards the caravans.

'Is that all?' asked Ida, 'I thought you said she could see into the future!'

'That's all,' replied Jal, 'She told you what she saw. She'd tell you more if there was more.'

Ida was disappointed. Every time she was excited at the prospect of finding the answers she was looking for, she ended up downhearted. It wasn't enough that she was all alone in this strange place, but try as she might, she just couldn't find her way out. She had no idea how to go back home, or even, if she ever would. She was stuck in a corner in a strange place she couldn't understand. Worst of all, there was no one to save her.

That night, Ida and Jal slept side by side, on the heath under the

Forget Me Not

stars. Ida was grateful to Jal and his family for having given her enough food to eat her fill, for the drinking water and for this magical night that she might never see anywhere else again. Jal may well be her best friend amongst all the people she'd ever met. How sad that she had to leave him and go away in the morning… If they lived nearby, they might meet every day. Jal could cheer her up with his accordion, and tell her how Tobar trains the birds.

But Ida knew this was impossible.

How enormous the sky looked from her bed on the heath! It looked infinite…

As dawn broke, they woke up and had breakfast. Since everyone was still asleep, everyone must be exhausted after last night's party. It was utterly silent, a little cool and fresh. It was time for Ida and her tulip to leave. Jal said they could stay if she wanted, but it was impossible. This wasn't Ida's home; at any rate, she had to replant her tulip back in her patch and then go back home. Jal gave her some food and water to take along. Ida was just about to put it all in her backpack, when she paused. She emptied it, and handed to Jal everything that was in it - except for her water bottle and blanket. He had been a real friend, even though they'd only spent one day together. He'd made her smile, and her tulip too; he hadn't even left them alone during their sleep. She had to give him a memento, and thought the stuff in her bag might please him. And anyway, she was now sure it made no sense to lug all that weight around.

'They all mean a lot to me. But I want to give them to you,' she said, as he handed them.

Jal was over the moon; he loved all of his presents. The pebbles would go at the head of his bed; he might even paint them in bright colours. And the pencil and paper? For his poetry, he exclaimed, hopping in place with excitement.

'I'll never forget you,' said Ida, 'Thank you for everything.'

'I hate good-byes. We'll meet again, anyway.'

'That's impossible; I'm going back home. But this is your home.'

Aslı Eti

'Like I told you, the earth is my home,' laughed Jal, 'You never know where we'll meet again!'

He'd opened both arms wide as if he would embrace the whole heath. Ida was reminded of something he'd said last night, before falling asleep. Jal had said, 'Nothing happens unless you dream of it.' It was a prayer Patia had taught him, one he recited every night before going to sleep, and that's how so many of his wishes had come true. Then he'd blown out an imaginary candle, closed his eyes and dived into the world of dreams. Having decided to say the same sentence every night from now on, Ida repeated them silently.

As the sun rose, the members of tribe woke up one by one. It was time to go. Jal wished the tulip a good journey, and advised Ida not to forget to compliment her flower. Beauty deserves tributes, he reminded her; she had to say something nice to her flower every day.

They hugged tight. But no amount of willpower could hide the tears from each other.

Then Ida set off for the misty mountain on the horizon, and Jal made for his caravan...

5

We're all free in reality.
Such a simple fact, yet we act as if we didn't know…

Ida walked non-stop for days and days and days, carrying her tulip, with the occasional break to eat or sleep. Every once in a while, she rested under a tree for a few minutes, no more. It was getting colder; winter had to be just around the corner. Ida was hoping to reach the peak before the frosts came, otherwise finishing their journey was going to be nothing short of a miracle.

The tulip was getting worse, with hardly any petals left; so many had dried and dropped off. She was coughing really badly and shivered at the first sign of a stiff wind. Ida frequently watered her and flattered her daily just as she'd promised Jal. All this helped cheer her tulip up a little, but wasn't enough to make her better.

One day, when Ida was carefully dribbling some water into the pot during a brief rest, the tulip spoke:

'Thank you, for refusing to give me to Fifika…'

'I'd never dream of giving you away. Don't even think about it.'

'Patia's tulip was lovely, though. Lustrous like I once was…'

'Just a pretty flower, that's all. But you are my friend. Of course, you may not want to be, and I couldn't blame you. It's my fault you're in this state… But as far as I'm concerned, you are my friend.'

'And you mine,' whispered the tulip in a trembling voice. Ida smiled for the first time since she'd parted from Jal, glad her tulip

Aslı Eti

had forgiven her! If someone had done to her what she'd done to the tulip, taken everything away, left her all on her own far from home, she would never forgive that person! Her tulip really did have a kind heart, just like the shepherd had said. Ida thought she'd done nothing to deserve forgiveness.

A few days later, they reached an ice-cold spring. Ida drank her fill, watered her tulip generously, filled her water bottle and decided to spend the night there. There was a hollow in a tree, just right to keep her tulip warm. Ida herself would have to make do with wrapping up in the blanket, huddling at the base of the tree. The nights were getting really cold now. She had to clench her little teeth all through the night. She was beginning to lose hope that she would ever reach the mountain.

The first thing she saw when she woke up in the morning was a bright white stork by the spring, quietly drinking water. Ida went over quietly so she wouldn't scare him away. She might have been spotted, but thankfully the stork didn't look alarmed. He was now cooling his wings in the water.

'Good morning,' he said, 'I tried to be quiet, seeing as you were sleeping, but...'

'Good morning,' replied Ida, 'No problem.' She then asked the stork where he came from and where he was going.

'From behind that yonder mountain. I have to go somewhere warm before it gets really cold.'

Ida couldn't believe her ears; she was so excited that she thought the ground was slipping from under her feet.

'Please tell me what's beyond that mountain? What's it like over there?' she asked, her heart pounding.

'The sky, forests, rivers, villages,' said the stork, 'Lots of lovely places...'

Ida's eyes shone: so she was on the right way! One of those villages had to be her own. She told the stork her tale in a flash: how she got lost, how she couldn't find her way back, and how she needed to go

Forget Me Not

beyond that mountain to get back home. The stork said his mustering had set off for warm lands before the cold weather set in (as he spoke, Ida congratulated herself for pretending to have always known the relevant collective noun: a *mustering* of storks!) but he had stayed behind. Because he couldn't fly! He'd tried, and many times; but his wings just couldn't keep him aloft. As soon as he rose up into the air, he came down with a crash. To be honest, he had lost all belief that these two wings could ever bear all his weight; he was scared to leap off from the mountaintop into the skies.

'So they had to leave me behind,' he carried on, 'Winter was approaching; they really couldn't wait for much longer.'

He told Ida about sitting in his nest for days and days, all on his own, thinking he could never fly. Until, that is, one day when a gigantic vulture attacked his nest.

'I jumped off in such a panic that I never even noticed I was soaring in the sky. I had no idea I'd be flying so high!' He gave a hearty laugh. 'In other words, I certainly realised I was flying. And the world looks more beautiful from above the clouds than I ever thought possible! Who knew!'

Leaving his nest for the first time and discovering other lands had blown his mind. He had discovered so many wonderful places on the way that instead of trying to catch up with his mustering, he'd decided to explore on his own.

'They must have got there by now. But I'm in no hurry. I'm having fun on this trip... And since I won't get back for quite a while, I might as well enjoy the scenery now.'

He said he'd be happy to take a short hop to the other side of the mountain; if Ida wanted, he would be happy to fly the sick flower there on his back. He couldn't offer to take Ida, since she was far too big and too heavy for him. Her heart fluttered all of a sudden. Instead of replying immediately, she whispered to her tulip:

'Do you want to go with him?'

There was a moment's silence. The only thing they could hear was the burbling of the spring and the wuthering of the wind. Ida was staring at the tulip on her lap. The poor thing resembled an ugly bald old man with a bent back, as drying leaves and petals were dropping off one by one. She really needed to get back to her patch straightaway. And that would also fulfil the foretold happy end. But Ida was scared witless at the thought of tacking the rest of the journey on her own. All the same, she knew her tulip needed to go back as soon as possible, and if the stork could take the tulip there, why not? Surely some kindly soul would be found to replant the tulip once they'd got there. All she had to do was get there. Tears streamed down Ida's cheeks at these thoughts. She wished she had a pair of wings to take her to the other side of the mountain with the stork and the tulip. There was nothing more she wanted just then.

After a brief pause, the tulip spoke in that velvety voice:

'I've thought about it, and I'm staying with Ida... If I went without her, I wouldn't be able to find anyone to plant me back in the soil. I'd be left all on my own.'

Ida sighed in relief. She couldn't believe her tulip wasn't going to leave her. She was free to go, yet she had chosen to stay. Planting a kiss on the slender stem, Ida said:

'I'll take you there as soon as possible, don't worry. Don't worry,' she felt the need to repeat her reassurance.

'All right,' said the stork. He would still fly over to the other side for a short spin; he could return to his mustering whenever he wanted, and he was thrilled at the thought of all those wonderful stories he'd tell them!

'Now you be careful, though,' said Ida, 'I don't want you to freeze or starve to death. There is a good reason why storks fly away before the winter, you know.'

'But I don't want to catch up with them!' exclaimed the stork, 'If we do the things we don't want to do, we lose the opportunity we've been given. We turn to creatures who always do what everyone else tells them to!'

He launched himself into the air, flew in a circle, and returned to exclaim merrily:

Forget Me Not

'Thankfully I've got wings to take me wherever I want!'

After a brief farewell he flew away. Ida and her tulip listened to the flapping as they watched his wings recede into a small white speck in the distance and vanish beyond the mountain.

Ida could hear her tulip sighing.

A pair of wings was the answer to so much.

6

You fail when you're afraid…
You're given a chance; don't waste it with your own hands.

The days were rushing by as Ida kept walking, carrying her tulip. Winter had set in; it was freezing day and night in the forest. When they finally reached the base of the mountain, they were too exhausted to feel glad.

One night the wind stiffened, whipping the branches of ancient trees into a frenzied lashing from side to side. Leaves blown up circled Ida, lashing her face and getting caught in her hair. Her frail tulip looked really poorly; she couldn't cope with the cold, and what few petals and leaves she had left didn't look like they'd survive such a storm. She wheezed so badly at night that Ida barely slept a wink, tucking the blanket around the tulip and giving as much water as she could to alleviate her suffering. Some nights, the tulip even spoke in her sleep. Ida couldn't make out what she was saying, but she kept pleading silently: *Please don't leave me!*

They'd been blown this way and that for days on the road, hardly getting much sleep, and now this storm was battering them even more! As if someone didn't want this journey to come to an end, as if someone kept putting obstacles in their way. But who could be so cruel? Ida kept repeating what Patia had said, kept trying to convince herself that they wouldn't die at the base of this misty mountain.

Forget Me Not

'You've got stars in your palms,' an assured Patia had announced, 'And this means you will eventually reach your goal.'

At night, Ida kept staring at her palms; but she couldn't see a single star. Worse still, there wasn't a single sign that she could find her way and reach her goal. Sometimes she thought it was all a bad dream, and the storyteller shepherd, the tree and Patia had all made fun of her. Terrifying thoughts. That's when her parents popped into her mind most. She really needed someone to ask what to do, just like she used to. Finding all the right answers all on her own, managing to climb to the peak of the mountain, and covering all this way and finally reaching home: all this sounded like fairy tales full of miracles that only little kids could believe in.

The wind grew stiffer, shaking the whole forest. *This must be a hurricane, I guess,* thought Ida. Unless she found somewhere safe to spend the night, this would be their end. She burst into sobs as she tried to walk on, blown one way and the other by the wind, crashing into trees. Scratched by the branches, her arms and legs and neck and face were covered in grazes. She could hardly keep her eyes open for all the dust and soil blown in the air; whenever she tried to open her eyes so much as a squint, dust pierced her eyes. Her frozen hands barely managed to keep hold of the flowerpot.

All of a sudden the forest was shaken by such a thunderous noise that thousands of screeching birds launched themselves up into the air. Then the skies opened: tonnes of water poured down. Ida had never seen rain like this before. It didn't seem to rain but spear the ground instead! She couldn't walk any farther; she fell onto her knees, trying to shield her tulip with her body. She huddled into the blanket to protect her head and body from the rain and the branches and pebbles blown everywhere. No amount of resisting the wind was any use. She'd tried to anchor herself to the ground by her nails, but the wind clutched at her and dragged her away. She banged her head a few times on the ground.

She must have lost consciousness, since she had no idea where she was when she next opened her eyes.

Aslı Eti

She was lying on the floor when she woke up. It was dim, except for the dozens of small flames like candles. It was a cold, stone floor she was lying on; the only thing she had for a mattress was a rough cloth like an aba. She noticed a damp rag on her forehead, and from what she could make out, her hands were still covered in scratches and grazes. Her eyes sought her tulip straightaway; she sighed in relief only after spotting when the pot right beside her. As she gathered her wits, she was gripped by fear. Where was she? How did she come to be here in this weird place? She tried to ask her tulip in a whisper, but the flower didn't reply - Ida hoped she was asleep.

Ida felt her whole body shivering in fear. The hairs on the back of her neck were bristling. She tried to move, but she was aching all over. She must have hurt herself quite badly as she was thrown about by the wind, and she had a headache. *I must have done the worst thing in the world to deserve all this,* she thought.

A voice broke into her thoughts.

'So you're awake! Hullo.'

She turned her aching neck towards the voice. An elderly man was coming over, carrying a bowl and a wooden spoon.

'You scared me, but thankfully you're all right.'

'Where am I?' asked Ida, 'Who are you?'

She wanted to look around to see what sort of place this was, but her fear and anxiety seemed to cloud her vision.

'You're in my home,' replied the old man, 'In a cave at the base of the mountain.'

The walls were of stone; the room really did look like it was carved out of rock. There was no light at all, unless you counted the feeble, trembling flames of the candles everywhere.

'You must have been dragged here in the storm. You were unconscious when I found you, and so was your flower...'

'So you saved us...'

Thanking him, Ida asked who he was and why he lived in a cave. Why would anyone do this all on his own in such a place? Was he also lost once, and failed to return home?

50

Forget Me Not

'I'm a sage,' he smiled, 'I wasn't lost, I'm here because I want to be.'

He told her to have a little bit of soup first; they could have a chat once she felt a bit better. Ida asked if her tulip was still alive, scared to death of hearing the worst.

'She is, don't you worry,' replied the sage, 'I must confess, however, I'd never heard of a snow tulip surviving so far from her patch. And given she's managed to survive this storm, too, we can safely assume a miracle's taken place.'

If the sage knew about the snow tulip, then all this had to be true. Somewhat reassured by his words, Ida had a few more spoonfuls of the soup before falling into an exhausted sleep.

She had no idea how long she lay there; but when she did open her eyes again, she felt much better.

'It took me days to reduce your fever,' said the sage, sitting, staring at her, 'Thankfully nature's generous enough to offer all the medicine we need.'

After sipping a little water from the earthenware bowl he handed out, Ida poured the rest into the tulip's pot. When she heard her breathing at long last, she said, 'Thankfully she's still alive.' She asked her tulip how she was, but there was no reply.

'She's still too exhausted to reply,' said the sage, 'But it won't take long for her to perk up, don't worry. If she can survive on a handful of soil, she can survive this too.'

This should have made Ida glad, but the sight of the tulip offered no heartening signs. It was totally bald now, not even a single petal! Those once dazzling snow-white, lustrous and velvety petals had vanished into thin air. Bent double, the stem had no shape left at all. It looked like it would blow away in the faintest breeze. Hard to believe this was a tulip. A sight that broke Ida's heart and stuck a lump in her throat; she didn't think she had any strength left to go on. They might never even leave this cave.

Moved by the pain on her face, the sage held her hand.

'Since she can't get any worse, she will get better from now on! Don't worry,' he said in an effort to set her mind at ease.

Aslı Eti

'How do you know?' snapped Ida, enraged by her own despair. She felt so tired, so lonely that there wasn't a single word that could comfort her.

'I'm a sage. It's my job to know.'

'Nonsense!' she blurted out, embarrassing herself at jumping down an elder's throat, and her rescuer at that! 'I mean, no one can know everything. Everyone only knows a little.'

No one had all the answers: neither the shepherd, nor the tree, neither Jal, nor Patia, neither the stork, nor the tulip, and least of all herself...

'Correct. I'm also aware I don't know everything.' His laughter rang on the dim walls. 'And I must confess, I'm a little surprised that you know that. Not many do.'

Ida told him her tale: how she got lost, why she set off, all that had happened on the way and everyone she met. She also admitted to having picked the snow tulip.

'I do know the prophecy, but... Maybe she doesn't like me any more, or doesn't like herself, maybe she's unhappy, and that's why she's getting worse. Why not?' she asked, her voice trembling. 'The prophecy says nothing about the tulip suffering so much...' She was scared to hear the sage's answer.

'Since she's survived so much, and is still resisting, no. I don't think so. She would have given up long ago otherwise.'

Ida wished he was right. Since he was a sage, he had to know best. She was going to ask for his help for her journey. But there was something else she had to know first. Why did he live alone in this mountainside cave?

'I was running away from storms,' replied the sage, 'They just wouldn't let up! I took shelter in this cave, and later just got used to it. This is my home now.'

'Are there so many storms around here then?'

'I was caught in so many hurricanes. And now I'm old, I can't possibly undertake such a long journey.' He was trying to light a couple of twigs in his hands to get a little fire going.

Forget Me Not

Ida wasn't convinced. It was winter now, yes, but spring would eventually come. There had to be days when the storm stilled. Even now, she couldn't hear any wuthering. Maybe it was calming down outside. You couldn't shelter in a cave for ever, could you?

'Are you scared of going out?' she asked. She didn't mean to embarrass him, but she was really curious. Why did he continue to live here? The sage didn't look in the least bit embarrassed when he replied, composed as ever:

'I've seen enough of the outside. I've got nothing to fear now.'

'All right,' said Ida, although she was still confused, 'How do you do what you do here... I mean, be a sage? All on your own?'

'Why not? A sage is a sage wherever he might be.'

'But if there's no one to hear you, what good is your ... sage-ness?'

'*Wisdom* is always good,' replied the sage more firmly, 'Even if you're alone.'

He may be right, thought Ida. She, too, was alone, and wisdom would certainly help her too.

'Can you help me?' she asked him, 'The storyteller shepherd told me to go to the other side of this mountain. Said that was the way home.'

'He was right. What else do you want to know?'

'Will I reach the peak? Will I succeed? Isn't all this impossible for a little child?'

'Nothing is impossible for a little child, so long as you know what you're looking for.'

'I do know what I'm looking for!' exclaimed Ida, of course she did. 'I'm looking for the way home; I want to find it as soon as possible.'

Just then the tulip gave a faint cough. Ida immediately turned and cradled her flower. She poured a little water from the bowl beside her, gently stroked the stem and asked how she was, but the tulip remained silent, probably fallen asleep again.

'As far as I can see, you're looking for your way back home, and keeping your tulip alive at the same time,' smiled the sage.

He was right. She wanted to do both.

Aslı Eti

'So what are you looking for?' she asked him.

'Something that was left under the bricks before I came here,' said the sage, his words almost lost in a guffaw mixed with a cough.

'What does that mean?'

'Since you ask,' said the sage and launched into his tale. When he was little, a flood had devastated his hometown, and his home was gone. So he was forced to migrate to a strange land, somewhere hard to get used to. He went hungry often and had to sleep on the streets on his own when he was building a house. There were many storms, he was cold, and he fell ill… Countless landslides demolished his house even before he had finished laying the bricks… Just when he was on the verge of losing all hope, he met the greatest love of his life: Lea! They met on a moonlit night, and were inseparable for years and years. Beautiful Lea had a marvellous voice, too lovely to ever forget. She was a travelling singer, who wandered from one place to another to delight townsfolk as that enchanting voice rang out in town squares. The sage stopped laying bricks night and day; wherever they went was home so long as they were together, and they travelled far and wide. He took up teaching, telling one town about the things he had seen and learnt in the previous. Townsfolk everywhere benefited from his teaching, and he was delighted to be of use, basking in admiration as people flocked to consult him on matters they wanted to know about.

They had a wonderful life, until, that is, Lea was struck by a serious illness and departed this life. All alone once again, the sage resumed laying bricks night and day again, not wanting to be left on the streets on his own. But he was dogged by bad luck: the autumn storms returned, and with them, rains, high winds, floods and landslides razed his house down. He grew old as he toiled endlessly. Thrown about by hurricanes, one day he took shelter in this cave, and never left since then.

'It's a very sad tale!'

'It sounds worse than it is. I had wonderful times too.' He began lighting the candles in his hand from the log fire. 'Except, I had forgotten what it was I was looking for all the time I spent laying bricks.' With another half-cough-half-laughter, he carefully arranged the candles on the walls.

'Will you be able to find it though, if you don't go back? If you don't lift the bricks and look underneath?'

'Of course I will!'

'Aren't you bored here?' asked Ida. She just couldn't get her head around how you could spend the whole day in this cave.

'Sometimes... but this is home.'

'Before I was blown here, I'd met a gipsy family on a heath in the forest. They played the best music in the world, wore colourful outfits and they were all poets...' Ida murmured one of the tunes she'd heard from Jal 'My mate Jal said the whole world was their home.'

The sage just gave a silent smile in response.

'And his grandma Patia can see the future,' Ida carried on, 'I think you two would get on great if you met her. Maybe she can tell you what you're looking for. She talks in riddles though; it's a bit hard to understand. But Jal's sure she knows the future, and I believe him.'

'She must do, if you believe him,' said the sage, before adding she had to sleep a little more, that she needed lots of rest to regain her strength. Ida stretched out on the aba. The flickering candle flames threw weird shadows on the walls. She watched them sleepily for a while. One looked like the kind tree she'd met first, another was the spitting image of the storyteller shepherd, and a third resembled her mother... She closed her eyes, silently reciting Patia's sleep prayer: Nothing happens unless you dream of it.

Ida was woken up by the tulip's sobs. The tulip was awake, her tears dripping like dewdrops onto the cave floor. She looked tiny, bent double in her pot. Cradling her at once, Ida asked, 'What's wrong?'

'I haven't got a single petal left! I'm totally bald!' screamed the tulip, choking in sobs, 'Just look at the state of me! I look sooo hideous...'

'No, no, no! You're not hideous!' Ida tried to speak without thinking, without even being glad at hearing the tulip talk again. The words hurt, but if she'd stayed silent, the tulip would only believe

Aslı Eti

it was out of shock at her ugliness. 'You're not hideous,' insisted Ida, 'Quite the opposite: you're my most beautiful friend.'

The tulip carried on sobbing. 'You're always flattering me. But I know it's not true. I can't bear to look this way.'

'Don't say that,' pleaded Ida, her eyes welling, 'It was an awful hurricane, and it dragged us here. Made us both sick. But look, we're still alive. And we'll get better.'

'Are you sure?'

'Sure I'm sure,' replied Ida, her voice strong and determined, 'You'll be just like you were once you return to your soil. I promise.'

The tulip's sobs calmed down a little. Just then the sage reappeared to stoke the fire; Ida pointed to him and told the tulip about all his help.

'He doesn't look at all happy,' whispered the tulip, 'He must have done something wrong.'

'Hush! He'll hear you,' chided Ida, 'We don't want to upset our rescuer!'

That's when the sage noticed their whispers and asked with a smile:

'I wonder what the legendary snow tulip has to say about me.'

Ida blushed as she replied with a bashful smile:

'Says you don't look that happy. And I don't think she's wrong either... I guess your knowledge doesn't make you happy.'

'On the contrary,' he replied, 'I am happy. Happy to be hosting you.'

They were startled by the tulip's shrill cry: 'Look at that!'

One of the countless shadows cast by the flickering candlelight was that of the tulip. Strangely, her shadow showed the tulip as she once looked: thick petals crowning an elegant, upright stem, as aristocratic as she used to be. Delighted at this unexpected promise of regaining her beauty, the tulip gazed at the image, looking as if she would never tire of the shadow on the wall.

'But how?' exclaimed Ida, 'How can your shadow be different?'

'It's perfectly possible,' said the sage, as if what he'd just seen was an utterly ordinary sight. 'The tulip might be ill and weak now... But in reality, she is a truly special and powerful flower. She's still filled

Forget Me Not

with kindness, with a pinch of all that is fine in the world. Why on earth not?'

Ida looked for her own shadow amongst the dozens on the wall. It was nothing like what she'd expected to see: it was tiny, looking really frail, bent double and hunched up. An image that filled her with fear.

'Oh... Do I really look like that?' she asked the sage.

He was staring at the shadow on the wall.

'You're ill, and you're run down. You're quite weak. But you will get better, don't worry.'

Ida wasn't at all happy with this tiny, weak and helpless state. How much harder must it be for her tulip to put up with her condition! Tearfully she asked the sage how she could get better at once.

'It could take quite a while,' he replied, 'You'll have to rest for months. Don't worry, though; you can stay here for as long as you like.'

Ida was panicking; she didn't really have that much time:

'I can't though! I have to find my way and return home as soon as possible. Anyway, my tulip can't possibly stay away from her patch for that long.'

'You'll fail if you go out in this state, though. You and your tulip... You can't reach the summit; it's impossible in your present state.'

'Please help us,' she pleaded. She had no idea what to do, and there was no one else who could help.

The sage was upset at Ida's state. Taking a deep breath, he spoke:

'There is a way to get better more quickly.'

Excited, Ida opened her eyes wide, exclaiming:

'What is it? Please tell me!'

She was prepared to whatever he was about to say.

'You have to show kindness to someone, make that person's life better. That's when you can get better and grow stronger.'

'But what can I do?' asked Ida hopelessly, 'You're the only person I can show kindness to, and I have nothing to give you.'

He didn't reply.

In silence, they finished their bowls of soup and retired to their corners, drawing their blankets over their shoulders. Ida felt totally

Aslı Eti

helpless. She was cornered for real this time. If only she knew what to do! She recited Patia's prayer in silence as she did every time she went to bed… and fell into an uneasy sleep in the dark cave.

When she woke up in the morning, the sage was sitting by her side. He seemed to be staring into the distance thoughtfully. After a few minutes of silence, he spoke of the narrow tunnel behind the cave. It led to the lands where he used to live. That was the only place it led to, nowhere else. If she wanted, she could come with him and help him carry some of the bricks of the house that was demolished. That would help him, and it would help her recover quickly.

'Wonderful!' yelled Ida, 'I can't thank you enough. I'll be the best brick carrier you've ever seen!'

To be honest, she was equally curious about what lay under the bricks.

They entered the tunnel: the sage, Ida and the tulip. The tunnel carved out of the rock was really narrow, and it was very dark. Firmly cradling her tulip, Ida said, 'Don't be scared.' She followed his footsteps. He told her not to hurry, and to mind her step.

The cave was so dark they could have been blind, so little could be picked out in the gloom.

It was such a bright day when they emerged from the tunnel that Ida was too dazzled to work out where they were. It took a while, but she eventually made out the pinkish sky, the colour of a hardboiled sweet. It looked lovely. Indistinct outlines in the distance spoke of the mountains on the horizon. Closing his eyes, the sage breathed in the air of his hometown.

Yellows and browns mingled with shades of red under the sky: all around them were adobe houses, one or two storeys high, all pretty alike, separated by flagstone streets. Several clearly ancient towers rose here and there. The streets were crowded with vendors, children, lambs and donkeys wandering everywhere.

They entered one of those narrow streets. Small markets popped up at virtually every step of the way, stalls in myriad colours: fabrics,

Forget Me Not

pots and pans, glass perfume phials and fresh fruit. The vendors were shouting in an unfamiliar language, pointing to their wares displayed on the brick walls and stone steps as they bantered with passers-by.

'It's not far… We're nearly there,' said the sage. And true enough, a few more steps and they were on the site of his never completed house: it was a ruin, nothing more than a heap of bricks. Taller than either of them, Ida thought it nearly reached the sky. The old roof was visible in the rubble.

The sun was beginning to set. Evening was drawing in.

Ida tried to lift the first brick, but it was far too heavy. It required a huge amount of effort just to nudge it. She decided to start with a smaller piece instead, picked another brick in the rubble and placed it to one side. She was delighted by her success.

Soon countless stars appeared in the sky, bathing the streets in glittering light. Ida could hear musicians and children's shouts from the back streets. This place looked like a happy family home.

The sage and Ida worked in starlight all night long. The tulip was sorry she couldn't help, but she enjoyed watching the stars, listening to the sound of music filling the narrow streets and dreaming of returning to her own home, to her patch.

A troupe of musicians walking past waved; a pretty woman danced and wished them luck. Then a strange man carrying a basket turned up. He gave Ida and the tulip a little show: he charmed an enormous snake out of the basket as he played on his flute. The creature danced for a while, bending this way and that, and then sank back into its basket. Ida kept working tirelessly, her excitement growing as the pile of bricks diminished.

The moon was like a gigantic mirror in the sky. It was a long night. Daybreak seemed a long way away, as if everything and everyone waited for Ida and the sage to finish.

They had a brief nap on the roof of the old house for a rest, and resumed working with all their strength.

Some bricks were very heavy, impossible for Ida to move. Only the sage was able to lift them, and sweating blood as he did so. He told Ida

Aslı Eti

that every brick had a memory. Some concerned very important days and events, and that made them much heavier. The day he saw Lea for the first time, for example, and the day they got married, and the day of the great storm, the day they had a massive row, the day Lea fell ill, and the day Lea departed this world…

He was struggling to breathe at times with the effort; his face went bright red and he was covered in sweat from top to toe. He hurt with every brick, Ida could see he was suffering, but he didn't grumble. He didn't say a word. He carried on lifting the bricks and placing them to the side one by one, without a break.

Hours later, the pile of bricks looked much smaller. The sage looked a little lighter on his feet as he had finished lifting the heaviest bricks.

All of a sudden, Lea's enchanting voice rose from the pile. It was a lovely, merry song, as if accompanying them. The sage was right. It was impossible to describe just how lovely her voice was. Ida and her tulip listened wordlessly.

There were only a few bricks left on the ground how. The sky was starting to lighten; soon the sun would rise. Ida lifted a couple more bricks and placed them at the side. When there was only one left, they both hesitated. Whatever it was that the sage had forgotten, it had to be under this brick. The sage steeled himself and lifted it. An ancient box appeared underneath: small, covered in dust.

He opened the box straightaway to reveal a shapeless stone of many colours, small enough to fit into the palm. His eyes lit up, brightening his face. He explained that this was a special healing stone; it was very rare, and only a few people in the world knew how to use it. This was a panacea, he said; it would cure all ills, and he was a young man when he'd learnt how to use it. (*Panacea,* thought Ida; here was another new word she'd just learnt!) He picked it up and stared. There was also a yellowed piece of paper in the box. He had written that note many years ago, at a time when he wandered from town to town as he taught. It said:

Start with others if you want to heal yourself

Forget Me Not

Pain can only be forgotten if it's eradicated from the face of the earth

'I'd totally forgotten about them!' exclaimed the sage ecstatically. As soon as he'd read the note, the pile of bricks they'd shifted all night crumbled into a handful of dust and was borne away on the wind.

The sage had found what he'd been looking for. He held his stone in his palm. He now knew what he had to do: he would stay in the town, resume teaching, and use his healing stone to help others. If there was no one left here who needed help, he would set off for another town.

'I couldn't have done it without your help,' he said as he gave Ida a hug.

'I couldn't have survived without your help,' replied Ida, gripping his hand.

He said they could stay with him if she wanted, but it was impossible. This wasn't Ida's home. She had to return home, once she'd replanted her tulip back in her patch first. Once she knew the tulip would get better and regain her former strength and glory.

Ida felt stronger somehow, even though she'd carried bricks for hours without sleep. He was right; she felt no weariness. The tulip seemed to be breathing more easily too, breathing more evenly by the sound of it. Clearly this place agreed with her. But now it was time to go back to the road. The sage wished Ida and her tulip well. Warning them about the cold weather that was around the corner, he said they had to be very careful, as their route would be covered in snow and ice. He then added:

'Don't forget: no one gives you a pair of wings when you fall off the edge. You have to build your own.'

Ida recalled the stork. Recalled how much she'd wished for a pair of wings (more than anything!) when the stork had offered to fly the tulip to the other side of the mountain. *What a strange coincidence,* she thought.

After a final farewell, Ida and her tulip entered the tunnel leading to the cave. She packed some food, water, a knife and some ointment just in case, and the aba she'd been sleeping on. This thick fabric

Aslı Eti

would protect them from the bitter cold of the mountainside. The tulip looked at her shadow for one last time, gazing at the thick, full head of petals, and graceful, upright stem.

'Don't worry,' said Ida, 'You'll soon regain your old strength. And you're still my loveliest friend just as you are.'

She stroked the stem gently as she made for the mouth of the cave.

When they had emerged, the cave crumbled into dust behind them, just like the sage's bricks. Ida and her tulip were left gaping at the motes of dust blown away by the wind.

7

You can't tame nature.
Neither inner, nor out.

The snow snuck in utter silence, painting the whole world a muffled white. It fell soundlessly day after day. Cradling her tulip, Ida pressed on, sinking in and out of this sparkling white blanket night and day. The base of the mountain was now behind her. Now she was climbing. A thick forest, steep rocks and relentless snowfall… Every time she raised her head to look at the peak, she felt dizzy. It looked impossibly high. And every time this happened, she made an effort to remember the storyteller shepherd's pasture where his sheep grazed. How impossibly far the mountain had looked when she was sitting next to him! Yet here they were, so this journey was clearly not impossible. Ida remembered his words often: 'Big things may not be as big as you think. They just like to look that way.'

It was white as far as the eye could see. Dozens, no, hundreds of crystals glittered on snow-covered branches. Ida had wrapped the tulip in a square of the aba she'd cut out so she wouldn't freeze. Despite all her care, though, the flower's cough seemed to be getting worse. Every morning she cried tears of dewdrops, dewdrops that had gathered on the bare stem and fell on the ground like the drops from a clear spring.

The snow cover grew thicker by the day. Sinking all the way into her knees at every step was slowing Ida down. It was getting harder

Aslı Eti

and harder to walk. Thankfully there was no wind or storm. Quite the opposite: so quiet and silent was nature that snow had not only covered the ground and the trees, but also drawn a thick duvet over the footfalls of every living creature. Even muffled their heartbeats.

Ida ate like a bird to conserve what little food she'd collected at the cave: there wasn't a single morsel to eat on the mountain now that all the fruit on the trees was frozen. Terrified, she forced herself to think of something else. So she murmured a song, or one of the poems she'd heard from Jal and his family.

Every once in a while a snowflake settled on the tulip's bare head, looking like a delicate jewel until it melted.

'Makes you look like a snow fairy,' said Ida, 'Snow really does suit you.'

'I guess there's no end to these compliments,' coughed the tulip, 'Jal had a smoother style, but thanks all the same.'

Ida wasn't going to stop complimenting her tulip, no matter how reproachful she might get. If she could bring a smile to the face of her only friend, that was great. It wasn't like there was anything else she could do for the tulip, after all…

She scouted out a tree hollow or a shallow cave to spend the night in… Tucked inside the aba, they tried to warm in each other's breaths. Ida knew how to light a fire, but damp branches just wouldn't catch. So their nights were spent in fitful sleep as they shivered, huddling close, willing the morning to come soon.

Evening was now falling early; it got dark all too soon. Ida was looking for a tree hollow to spend the night. But they were in an opening; fewer trees made it harder to find somewhere to sleep in. Unless she found shelter before darkness set in, they might not make it till the morning.

Then she spotted a tall tree with a thick trunk, took a few steps and froze on the spot, her eyes locked on two blue dots twinkling a few metres ahead. Spots also locked on her eyes, looking as if they were watching her without moving a muscle. Not even daring to breathe, Ida stood like a statue in the snow.

Forget Me Not

'Do you see it too?' she whispered.

'Yes,' replied the tulip, her voice trembling.

'Don't you dare cough,' cautioned Ida, 'Please don't make a sound.'

That face off lasted for a few minutes. Then those bright blue dots moved quick as a flash, springing towards Ida and the tulip. Ida had no time to think. Her mind was made up in less than a second: she leapt up to the ancient tree beside her, taking the branches in twos. She climbed without looking back, her hands and feet slipping on the icy branches. Snow crystals were piercing her palms as icy branches slashed her fingers. Her hands were so numb that she couldn't feel her fingers any longer. It was really hard to grasp anything; she came close to falling several times when she lost her balance and stopped herself by grabbing a branch at the very last moment and she dragged herself up again. Just when she was close to the top, still moving from branch to branch, the flowerpot slipped from her hand. 'Noooo!' she yelled. The owner of the two bright blue spots stood at the bottom of the tree, still as a statue, looking up at her. Powerful and proud. It was a snow-white wolf.

Her tulip lay on the ground at the wolf's feet. Ida had to pick her up at once; the poor tulip couldn't stand the cold. It would freeze there and then.

'Please go away!' she yelled at the wolf, 'Please!'

As if it hadn't heard, the white wolf waited without moving a hair, still as a marble statue. Those eyes never left Ida for a moment. Ida considered shooing it away by hurling a big branch. But those thick branches were impossible to break off, slippery as glass in the frost. She tried to break off one of the icicles hanging down. It was no use. They were too thick to break. And her fingers were numb with the cold anyway... She could barely use her hands. Even breathing on them wasn't enough to warm her fingers. It was obvious she could do nothing to rescue her tulip from her perch. She had to get down. There was no other way.

But getting down meant death. The other option was to wait in the tree. No one could tell how long that would take. Minutes, hours,

Aslı Eti

maybe even days... Neither Ida, nor her tulip could stand it. Ida knew for certain that the wolf was the toughest of them all. There was no escape this time. She started trembling with fear, crying quietly as the tears froze on her eyelashes. How foolish of her to convince herself of miracles! She was condemned the moment she'd picked the tulip, and obviously she would have to pay. No one could predict where this journey would lead: not the shepherd, not the tree, not Jal, not Patia, not even the sage. No one. That's what the prophecy said. Ida couldn't believe this was going to be her end. She clenched her jaw so tight that her chin was shivering. 'Please, oh please!' she whispered over and over.

Night had fallen; it was totally dark. Ida shut her eyes tight, knowing full well opening them meant facing the blue eyes of the white wolf. She thought she could hear the tulip's silent sobs. Or maybe her body was beginning to freeze, and her senses were tricking her. Was her tulip dying? Was that her choking to death? Ida didn't want to see it; it would be far too painful to bear. She would keep her eyes shut for ever. She had no idea how to come out of this nightmare. The worst thing was, the real nightmare began when she opened her eyes.

Suddenly she felt a breeze. It was a familiar sensation; she'd felt the same thing on their first night in the forest, when they were sheltering in the tree. As if the tree's leaves were stroking her hair... That's when she heard the whisper from somewhere deep down:

'Bring your flower here... Otherwise it will die.'

'Was it you who spoke?' asked Ida, touching a snow-covered branch. Her eyes were still shut tight.

'Yes, of course,' said the tree, 'Who else! Go on, go get it.'

'I can't! I'm scared.'

'Go on,' said the tree, 'She's scared too... Open your eyes and take a look at your tulip! If you keep your eyes shut like this, you can't see what state she's in.'

'I know,' whispered Ida, pointing to the wolf, 'But I'll be attacked

Forget Me Not

if I go down. It's waiting for me. And I can't even grip the branches. My fingers are really numb, and my hand can feel nothing.'

'You have no choice. You can't wait in fear for ever. Don't worry, by the way: if you do the right thing, nature will help you.'

Ida wasn't at all convinced by this piece of advice. All the same, she knew she couldn't wait in fear for days and days.

'She has no one else but you. You have to do it,' said the tree gently.

Ida opened her eyes a little, trying to pluck up her courage. Two bright blue dots were still glowing in the same place, and her tulip lay at the wolf's feet... Lying flat. The wolf wasn't interested in the tulip though. It wanted Ida.

'She has no one else but you,' repeated the tree in a whisper. Then a light breeze caressed Ida's neck.

Ida wiped her tears and stared at the branches below her. One looked quite close. She hopped down. She carried on climbing down by hopping from one branch to another. There were only a few branches between the wolf and her now. The wolf bared its fangs, its growling ripping the silence.

The tree whispered again:

'It's now or never.'

Staying securely on this branch, Ida asked the wolf:

'What do you want from me?'

'Everything's under snow. I can't find any food,' growled the wolf. 'I have to eat. More importantly, my cubs are hungry. They're all waiting for food.'

'Please leave me alone!' screamed Ida.

'I can't! You're my only hope tonight. All the animals have retired for the night, all my prey's hiding in their holes and burrows and warrens. There's nothing else... I can't let my cubs starve to death.'

'But I have to fetch my tulip,' said Ida tearfully, knowing full well the wolf wouldn't let her off.

'This? This puny weed, you mean?' said the wolf, looking at the poor flower lying at her feet.

'It's not a puny weed!' exclaimed Ida, 'On the contrary, she's quite

Aslı Eti

special. She'll freeze if she stays there. I must fetch her as soon as possible. I can't let her freeze to death.'

'Come and get her then,' grinned the wolf, her eyes never leaving Ida for a fraction of a second.

Ida knew this was a trap. When it came to survival, no one spared anyone else. She thought of the cubs waiting for food, and she took another look at her tulip about to freeze on the snow. How much easier it would all be, she thought, if only everyone didn't just think of number one first! Just as she thought there was no way out, she spotted the red speckles on the snow. The white wolf was wounded. She was bleeding.

'You're hurt!' said Ida quietly, 'Let me help you.'

Brushing off the offer, the wolf repeated icily, 'I have to feed my cubs. I have no other choice.'

'Then we'll all die,' said Ida firmly enough to surprise herself, 'You, me, my tulip and your cubs... All of us. This makes no sense at all. Stop being so obstinate, and let me help you,' she carried on, 'Then you'll live to mind your cubs. I'll heal you, and you can spare me in return.'

'OK,' said the wolf after mulling over this proposal. Swift as lightning, Ida hopped down, grabbed her tulip and climbed back up to secure the pot in the crook of a branch. She rummaged in her backpack, grabbed the ointment and climbed back down. She applied it liberally to the deep wound before climbing back up and settling down for the night on one of the higher branches. Tucking her tulip into the aba she wrapped around herself, she tried to warm the flower up with her breath for a while.

'You saved her,' whispered the tree, 'You're a true friend.' Tenderly the branches curled around Ida, creating a warm snug against the cold.

Ida couldn't believe her eyes, but made herself a pillow out of leaves anyway and closed her eyes. She felt her heart beating at the same time as the tulip's did. She felt she belonged to a totally different world, far from home. Staying on this tree with her tulip meant she wasn't the little girl in the village. Some things had vanished for ever in this strange forest.

The tulip's heartbeat had steadied. She thanked Ida quietly: she was grateful for the rescue, even if it meant Ida had endangered her own life.

'How could I leave you to die?' asked Ida, 'I could never do that!'

The tulip spoke of the times when she was still in her own patch; her only worry then was losing her beauty. How she'd enjoyed enchanting everyone who saw her. 'I used to think I couldn't live if I'd lost my beauty,' she carried on, 'I was absolutely sure. But I was wrong.'

Everything happened too fast and everything changed too quickly. Days and nights sped by. Now the tulip was glad she'd survived. She told Ida about the shadow on the sage's wall; it just wouldn't leave her mind:

'So my old beauty must be there somewhere, since that was definitely my shadow.'

'Of course it is,' said Ida, hugging the pot.

They stayed like that for a while, eyes shut; then, reassured by each other's company they fell asleep.

When Ida woke up and glanced at the wolf at the bottom of the tree, she thought the wound looked like it was healing. She decided to climb down and check. The white wolf stayed still as Ida climbed down from branch to branch. Ida took a few steps.

Then the wolf shot like an arrow! With a ferocious growl, she tried to sink her fangs into Ida; her promise had clearly been forgotten. The more Ida tried to free herself, the heavier the wolf settled on her, fixing the girl under her paws. As they grappled, they sprayed snow all around.

All of a sudden a roar rumbled through the forest. The noise was coming closer, getting louder and louder. In the blink of an eye, a gigantic avalanche arrived, pouring over the snow, groaning as it dragged Ida and the wolf to the depths of the forest.

When things calmed down once again, Ida saw the wolf cubs rush to their mother. That's when she spotted the wound: it had opened

Aslı Eti

again, and it looked far worse this time. It must have happened when the wolf was tossed around by the avalanche. Bleeding buckets, the wolf lay in her death throes in a puddle of her blood. She was panting now, her groans echoing through the forest. Ida didn't think the wolf could last much longer, and she had no idea what to do.

Wild beasts appeared one by one, drawn to the smell of fresh blood. They gathered around for this unexpected feast. The cubs were frantically running around their mother, trying in vain to attack the other beasts.

Ida ran away, worried about the cubs and their loss in this eerie forest. Now they were all alone too. They were all left without shelter too.

Ida returned to the tree and cradled her tulip. She mourned the sad end of the white wolf, all the while thinking of her own mother - who must have done everything to find *her* daughter.

Later, as Ida trudged through the snow on her way to the peak, sinking in with each step, thoughts lined up in her mind, refusing to be stilled. She tried to comfort herself. She tried to shake off the horror she'd just witnessed. Staring at the tulip in her hand, she kept repeating the same thing over and over again:

'We're not alone; we can't be.'

8

You're not who you think you are.
You don't know who you are.
But you do know that you don't know who you are.

Spring had finally arrived. Stiff winds and storms were well behind them and the sun shone generously. Halfway up the mountainside now, Ida and her tulip were hoping the rest of the journey would be much easier. The snows were melting, and the burbling brook that ran alongside cheerfully promised plenty of water. They had survived a whole winter on whatever the ground had given Ida to eat; and soon the trees would burst into fruit.

Throughout that long trek, the tulip frequently talked of the old days. She might still wake up at sunrise and shed a few silent tears, but Ida thought reminiscing might actually be making her happy. The tulip went on and on about sipping the raindrops, she and her neighbours, and sheltering in the stiff winds by leaning on one another. About watching the sunset and the stars together and imagining what it would be like to follow a butterfly that had landed on their petals. Of course, it had never even occurred to her at the time that she might be picked one day and travel so far… She might have dreamt about leaving home, although that was just an idle dream at the time. It was all a bit of fun, like a fairy tale that would never come true. Ida, on the other hand, had never even imagined anything like this, thinking the whole world consisted of her own home. She

Aslı Eti

recalled her astonishment at Jal's claim of having lots of homes all over the world.

Ida was getting tired; she had to find somewhere for a brief rest. That's when she spotted what looked like huts on a hill in the distance. She hurried towards the hill. If they really were houses, she might get some food there.

A long trek proved her right: it was a tiny mountain village! Ida counted five houses on the slopes. A tiny, secluded village of no more than five houses. On their way to one, Ida and the tulip spotted the children running towards them. Five boys chattered merrily as they approached. They mostly looked about the same age, a couple were a little younger, but the rest were her age at the most. They had dark, curly hair and strikingly huge, bright eyes. Their outfits could best be described as simple robes of thin material, and their feet were bare. They all wore several colourful wristbands in different designs.

'Hi!' the boys said, waving as they ran towards Ida, 'Welcome to our village!'

'Hi!' said Ida, and introduced herself and her tulip.

'A tulip?' asked the youngest, astonished. He couldn't keep his eyes off the flowerpot in Ida's hand. He circled, peered again, and then brought his head as close as he could to the tulip's slender stem.

'A real tulip, eh? But it has no petals; it just looks like a dry twig...'

Knowing this would really upset her tulip, Ida told him not to say that; she explained that this was a special snow tulip, and her best friend to boot.

'It's sick, this tulip,' said one of the older boys, 'I might be able to help.'

'Can you really?' exclaimed Ida. Her surprise was clear to see.

'Of course he can,' said another boy, 'That's his talent. He's got healing hands. He can heal the sick.'

'Really? Wonderful! I'd be so happy if you could examine my tulip.'

'With pleasure,' replied the boy, carefully picked the pot and peered as if examining the flower. But his face fell at once.

Forget Me Not

'What's wrong?' asked Ida, dreading the worst.

'This tulip was picked from her patch against her will,' replied the boy, 'Which has done her no good at all. Made her very weak.'

Ida told him her story. Told him she was taking the tulip back to her patch. Every time she had to repeat her story, she felt sadder, unable to look her tulip in the eye. And every time it reminded her of her regret, and forced her to confess to that shameful mistake... Strangely, she also felt a little better every time.

'That wasn't great,' said the boy, 'All I can do is give her a little bit of strength. I can't do any more.'

He touched the stem gingerly. The tulip felt much better at once. She took a few deep breaths and thanked the boy in her velvety voice.

Hearing the tulip speak, the youngest boy exclaimed:

'A talking tulip! So that's her gift then!'

'That's right,' smiled Ida, 'I said she was very special.'

The boy cradled the tulip and started asking questions. The tulip replied graciously: where she came from, what she used to look like, what did she like doing best, did she have any friends... The tulip was delighted at being the centre of attention after all this time, delighted at seeing some stranger's eyes light up at the sight of her. The boy also enjoyed their chat; he wouldn't let go of the tulip, not even for a moment.

Ida turned to the boy who'd pepped up her tulip a moment ago and asked how he did it.

'Like my mates said; that's my gift. Healing the sick. Everyone in our village has a gift.'

He then introduced himself and his friends. His name was Boika, well, Boikany in full, but Boika for short. It meant *healer*.

'This is Mawa,' he said, pointing to one of the younger boys, 'He has the voice of an angel. You'll sing for our guests later, eh, Mawa?'

'Of course!' exclaimed the boy whose name meant *voice of an angel*, 'With pleasure!' Ida couldn't wait to hear him sing.

'And this is Kafintan,' said Boika, pointing to a third boy, 'He's a great carpenter. He can build whatever you can think of. Statues,

Aslı Eti

tools, all kinds of furniture… Whatever you want. There's nothing he can't build or mend.'

Like all the others, his name also described his gift. Names were given according to gift in this village. The fourth boy was called Mai, again, short for the proud name of Mai Tseren Gudu: fast runner.

'No one can outrun him in the whole forest,' continued Boika, 'Grampa says he's faster than even a hound.'

'And what about his name?' asked Ida, pointing to the youngest who was still talking to the tulip.

'That's Magariba.'

'What does his name mean? What's his gift?'

'He doesn't know yet,' said Boika, 'And since he doesn't, no one else does either.'

'He says he has no gift at all,' interrupted Mawa, 'That's why he's unhappy.'

Boika chided him:

'Don't say that! Or he'll only end up convincing himself he has none.'

'So what does Magariba mean then?' asked Ida curiously. Since all the names in the village denoted a skill, this name also had to mean something.

'Magariba means twilight. The darkness before sunrise,' replied Boika.

Ida felt a shiver. She watched the cheerful boy with the lovely huge bright eyes chatting to her tulip. His name didn't suit him at all.

'Why was he given such a name?' she asked, 'A bit gloomy, isn't it?'

'Not at all!' chuckled Boika, 'It's great. The darkest moment just before sunrise, when no star is visible, nor the moon. A child who's called Magariba is considered to be unborn in our village. He'll be born once he finds his calling.'

Ida didn't quite understand what Boika meant. How could you consider a child who was already born as an unborn?

'All children are called Magariba at first. They acquire their true names once they know who they are and what they can do. They

Forget Me Not

choose their own names,' explained Boika, 'Since we believe in our village that you are known by your work in this world. Simple, really...'

The more she thought about it, the better and simpler she found this custom: if you ran fast, you were called *Runner*; if you healed people, then your name spoke of your healing hands... Everyone in the village had a job, a gift. Which meant all villagers did what they were best at so they might benefit everyone else in the village. And that wasn't all. A child who found his name also got one of the stars above: the village believed that every star belonged to a child, and shone only for that child. When the child grew up into an adult, grew older and waved good-bye to life this time, the star also dimmed. When he was born again, his star was also reborn. So all children had a star of their own, and it was for ever... All they had to do was find their name and claim their star.

'Why hasn't Magariba found his gift yet? What's he going to do then? Isn't he going to claim his name or star?'

'Of course he will,' replied Boika firmly. It would have been unthinkable otherwise. Every child unquestionably had a star above. Unquestionably.

'He just can't find it here, in the village,' he carried on, 'He has to go to the other side of the mountain to discover his gift. Which means fording the stream first. Of course, we'll all go too; we'd never leave him alone.'

Ida glanced at the stream, a pure white froth burbling alongside. A full, wide river at this point, reaching all the way to the base of the mountain on the endless green plain. Huge, pointy boulders rose up all the way. Crossing the stream meant fording the river by walking over these boulders. These pointy boulders, sharp enough to tear feet to shreds...

'Exactly!' said Mai, 'Our feet would be torn to shreds if we tried to ford the stream.'

'Have you ever tried?' asked Ida.

'Not yet,' replied Boika, 'We need a pair of shoes each. And we

Aslı Eti

have such a long way to go after the stream too. We can't make it without shoes.

'That's why we are making them,' said Mai, telling her about the sandals they'd been weaving out of thick rope for four seasons. Robust sandals woven out of yucca fibres to protect their feet on their journey; four of the boys already had theirs.

'We can't set off before the fifth is ready though,' exclaimed Boika.

'Whose is the fifth?' asked Ida.

'Magariba's,' said Mai, 'We'll be all set as soon as his sandals are finished.'

'But we have to hurry; in fact, we don't have a minute to waste!' continued Boika gravely, 'Spring's arrived, the snows are melting so quickly, and that snowmelt's running into the stream. Soon the waters will rise. Only a day or so, and the stream will be too full to cross,' he added, staring at the frothing waters. Anxiety shone on his thoughtful face as he explained that it was impossible for Magariba to remain nameless and starless for one more season. Those sandals had to be made, no matter what, and Magariba had to cross to the other side before the waters rose to reach the mountain.

'I can help,' said Ida, 'We can weave much faster. I'm quite good at weaving, you know.'

'Great!' said Mai, 'Would you really help us?'

'Of course I would. And then I'll carry on my way.'

She asked why the others with the sandals had not set off ahead: they could easily cross the stream and chart their path, also serve as an advance party and even gain some time.

'Impossible,' said Boika, 'We can't leave Magariba behind. If we're one short, we're incomplete.'

'Yes, but you're always together. Just a couple of days... What difference would it make?'

Her tulip had been away from her patch all this time, and Ida had been far from her village... They would go back and pick up where they'd left off, wouldn't they? Ida thought Boika was making a big thing of this. A few days wouldn't change everything for ever, would it?

Forget Me Not

"Course it would!' said Mai, 'Just think: can you have a tree without a trunk, branches or roots? I mean, we can't do it if we're not together. We'll go together.'

'And there's no point in an advance party,' said Boika, 'We can't find what he's looking for. We don't even know where to look. He has to find it himself.'

So they sat down to weave a pair of sandals for Magariba. They carried on working in the bright moonlight after the sun had set. Ida was making the rope out of the fibres first, and then they all worked on making the sandals. They worked non-stop until the first light of day. Sleepless, exhausted, yet not caring about their own needs, worked and worked.

But there was a huge problem: as fast as the sandals were made, they unravelled! No matter what the children did, how tight and sturdy they made them, the sandals just kept unravelling. Ida gave a tearful look at her bleeding, blistering fingers, and then stared at the tiny sandal in her hand that she just couldn't finish...

'It's been days, no, weeks; and we still can't finish these sandals,' blurted Mai, 'Nothing works. Not even Kafi's skilful hands. It's the same thing again, we're just never going to finish them...'

'Of course we will,' Boika interrupted him, 'Absolutely we will. We're missing something though; I wonder what it is?' He asked that in a murmur, almost to himself.

Sitting in silence, they watched the rising sun. Ida kept weaving with the rope in her hand, but she'd lost hope of finishing the sandals. There had to be a problem; that must be why the kids had failed to finish the sandals for months and months.

That's when a timid voice broke the silence:

'You're not missing anything. It's me. I just haven't got the courage to set off, that's all,' said Magariba in a trembling voice. He tucked his head between his knees and hid his face. His friends had been working night and day for months to finish his sandals, and he'd been too scared to tell them the truth. How can you set off if you can't even admit your fear to yourself? It was impossible.

Aslı Eti

'Now we know,' said Boika. It was a huge problem. If Magariba didn't want to go, this journey just wouldn't happen. Until he gathered his courage and decided to go, there would be no journey. That's why the sandals refused to be made. Boika said they'd been busy with the wrong thing all this time; the first thing to do was to encourage Magariba. That's what real friends did. The sandal would follow as soon as Magariba gathered his courage.

They tried to buoy him up all day long. Each boy reeled off one encouraging and inspirational sentence after another. He listened avidly, but Magariba didn't seem all that impressed. He didn't look particularly braver either. Quite the opposite, he looked sad and dejected, sitting as week as a patient who hadn't left his bed for days; despair was plain on his face. Every once in a while he took the tulip on his lap; he only chatted to her. Asking her how she managed to stay brave despite being so far from her patch. And whether she was sure she would get back... 'I'm sure,' soothed the tulip in her velvety voice, 'I know I'm going back home... And who says I'm not scared? Sometimes I'm more scared than you could imagine. But courage isn't about not being scared. Courage is carrying on walking in this forest even if you're scared to death. If we make it to the summit, we will make it home. We have no other choice.'

Hours passed as the boys waited for Magariba to make his mind up. As soon as possible... Before the river rose too high... But Magariba didn't make a sound. He stood silent, too ashamed to look his friends in the face. They were all ready, waiting to help him, but he just couldn't make that first move. Never mind gather his strength, he pondered about the fear inside that he just couldn't rip out. Since he had never left the village before, he had no idea of the perils waiting on the other side of the mountain. Even the grown-ups in his family had all chosen to live quietly in the village. Not a single one had ever ventured outside. Of course, they'd all found their gifts without having to embark upon such an undertaking... Lucky for them! Magariba was sure he wouldn't survive if he had to take to the road on his own at this young age.

Forget Me Not

Then evening fell, and the stars glittered into view one by one. Soon the moon appeared and the sky above was filled with bright stars.

'Look,' said Boika, pointing at the sky, 'So many stars! Yours is somewhere there too, you know.'

An abashed Magariba lifted up his gaze to the sky.

'It looks so near, but it's so far in actual fact...' he sighed, 'Perhaps I'm just ordinary... Perhaps I have no gift to discover or anything...'

'No one is just ordinary,' interrupted the tulip confidently, 'Don't you dare let go.'

The river would be higher the next day. Magariba knew he couldn't possibly wait for another year. He was on the verge of losing his last chance to find his name and his star. An enormous upset for his family, friends and his village, and all because of him.

He whispered to Ida and the tulip:

'All these people in the village, and I'm the only one who had to undertake such a journey. Why? Why can't everything be as easy for me as it was for them all?'

Ida was at a loss for something to say. She was sorry for Magariba. The only thing she could think of to cheer him up was Patia's prayer that Jal had told her about. It had worked for her that night of the wedding, and it might work for Magariba.

'Nothing happens unless you dream of it,' she said. She told Magariba about Patia and Jal, and advised him to repeat it a few times every night before going to sleep. His wish might come true then.

Taking her counsel, Magariba closed his eyes. He took a deep breath, repeated the sentence a few times and fell asleep.

He dreamt he was on his own star, standing on a high hill. His star was telling him something:

'Look; you can see the whole world from here.'

What stretched out before him was space: an infinite fabric of planets and galaxies. He looked at the earth spinning in there somewhere. He, who had never seen anywhere outside his village

Aslı Eti

could now see the whole world in one go! It shone, a blue globe in the void.

That's when a rope appeared at his feet. A long and slender rope...

'Take this rope,' said the star, 'It's the longest one in the world. Tie one end to the tree there, and the other to your waist. Don't be scared, just let yourself go into the void.'

Magariba glanced at the old tree behind him, and then at the abyss at his feet. It looked so deep. Dark, empty space fell away below him. How could he possibly drop off into this precipice?

'This is an invisible rope; it becomes invisible the moment you leap,' continued the star, 'But it will always be at your waist, and you will always know it's there. So you'll be able to wander around the world with no fear. Everything you've got to discover is there. Just waiting for you.'

The earth looked dizzyingly beautiful, beckoning Magariba, a pull that was too hard to resist. Magariba couldn't keep his eyes of it. With barely a moment's hesitation, he gathered his courage, tied one end of the rope to the tree, and the other around his waist. Giving the star a cheery, 'Ta ta for now!' he walked off the edge, shouting as an afterthought, 'See you soon!' as he took his first step into the void.

The star's voice echoed in the void:

'This invisible rope always keeps me beside you, don't forget!'

Magariba could feel the wind blowing through his hair, chilling his cheeks and neck as he fell in the void. There was no wind in space, and you couldn't hear sounds either. He must have entered the earth's atmosphere then. He kept falling fast. Everything sped past his gaze before vanishing: the sky, the sun, the moon, the stars, and the clouds.

With a gasp, he opened his eyes.

It was morning; the sun was just rising. Everyone else was asleep. It was totally still. Magariba was the only one on his feet. He got up, washed his face in the icy cold stream and took deep breaths in the fresh air. Now he was sure he would cross the stream. He had made his mind up. He patted his waist, recalling the invisible rope between him and his star. Impatiently he woke everyone up and spoke about

Forget Me Not

his dream in the twinkling of an eye. They were all delighted that he had finally made his mind up.

Magariba was all excited now; he wanted to put his sandals on and cross the stream straightaway. The waters had been rising all night long and the river would be impossible to ford in a few hours. He announced to all present, that is, the boys, Ida and the tulip, everything he had to discover waited for him on the other side of the mountain. Perhaps he had to become an explorer to find what he was looking for. Perhaps that was his gift: an explorer who discovered the world! Why not; explorers were also gifted. All he had to do was to start exploring.

Ida and the boys immediately started weaving the fifth pair of sandals. Her poor, battered hands developed calluses as her fingers bled. But they all carried on, ignoring the aching wounds. Magariba had made his mind up, so it was impossible for him not to set off. These sandals would be finished before the water rose, come what may.

Magariba's sandals were ready by the time the sun had peaked overhead. He put them on his feet and patted his waist to make sure his invisible rope was still there. Everything was ready. They could set off. The boys gathered at the riverbank and thanked Ida and the tulip for all the help. Gingerly touching Ida's hand and the tulip's slender stem, Boika offered them strength, so they could come to the end of their journey as soon as possible and get home safe and sound. He also gave her a lucky charm as they called them in their village: one of the several a colourful wristbands adorning his arms. They hugged.

Mawa sang a merry tune before they set off. Enchanted by his lovely voice, Ida dreamt of an imaginary band, the most wonderful in the world: Mawa's song and Jal's accordion. They could travel and perform wherever they wanted. Who knows, they might get together one day...

Losing friends all the time was painful, thought Ida. Would she ever have the chance to meet people after she'd gone back home? She didn't know. Everyone she met, made friends with, and grew to like seemed to vanish like dust in the air. She couldn't hang on to anyone,

Aslı Eti

she just had to leave them behind and carry on. There was so much in this life that she used to think was hers, and was just beginning to realise belonged to no one. Never mind friends; not even the air, water, trees, wind all the rain belong to anyone. Ida wondered why she'd never noticed that before.

And now the boys were crossing the stream, fording that powerful flow. Thankfully she still had her tulip. She hugged the flowerpot, her eyes fixed on her friends until they reached the other bank.

Deciding to spend the night by the stream before starting out at daybreak, Ida settled under a tree with her tulip and watched the stars.

She wondered if she had a gift she had yet to discover. She must have come to this world to do some good. Before closing her eyes to go to sleep, she thought one of the stars above was shining for her.

9

If a handful of soil,
a little air and
a drop of water can give birth to a forest,
then everything is possible on Earth.

Spring had given way to a hot and dry summer. The searing sun bleached the weeds and other plants as the parched soil cracked under the evaporating puddles – what little was left, that is. Ida kept walking non-stop, carrying her tulip. She had made good progress in the soft, warm spring weather, climbing higher and higher. They were closer to the peak than ever before.

But the dry season meant finding water was a major problem now. She was having to count the drops she sipped from her water bottle just as she had done at the start of her journey. The riverbed was way behind them now; all she could find was the occasional small puddle.

The tulip wasn't doing that well. She had perked up a little in the spring, although not as well as the other flowers that blossomed robustly. As the prophecy had said: only her own soil could save her. She was exhausted like never before in the dry heat. She only spoke once every few days now, her breathing was really laboured and she spent the majority of the day sleeping. Ida repeated her silent pleas, *We've come all this way, please hang in there, please!* They were so near the peak, of course she wasn't going to abandon her tulip here, now

Aslı Eti

they were so close; they would complete this journey no matter what. They had to believe it. They had no other choice.

One evening, revived by a cool breeze, the tulip asked in a whisper, in a dreamy voice as if talking in her sleep:

'Do you remember Magariba's dream?'

'Yes,' replied Ida, 'I do...'

'Remember the invisible rope between him and his star?'

'I do.'

'We have such a rope too. We're fastened to each other by an invisible rope. Even if we don't feel it when we touch, even if we don't see it when we look, that rope is always between us...'

'Absolutely,' agreed Ida, 'We're fastened for ever by that rope.'

She gave her tulip a soft kiss on the stem and prayed silently with all her heart. Prayed that the tulip wouldn't vanish into thin air like all the other friends she'd made on this journey.

On that endless climb to the peak, they felt as if they were rationing their breath in the dry heat as beads of sweat trickling down their foreheads evaporated before long.

One morning, Ida thought she couldn't hear her tulip's breath at all. She listened carefully, waited a little and pressed her ear to the stem once again. There was no sound. She tried talking, asking if the tulip could hear her. Not a peep. Ida looked in her water bottle straightaway: there were only a few drops left. She had been walking for hours without drinking a single drop in this exhausting heat. There was no way these few drops could save them, and there was no water as far as the eye could see. Ida felt she was losing all her strength, as if she would faint then and there. Her hands were shaking and she felt dizzy. It was obvious they couldn't go on. Maybe this was simply the end. Maybe neither Patia, nor the sage had told the truth. Never mind reach the peak, she couldn't take another step. She just collapsed on the spot. She stretched out on the cracked soil. Maybe closing her eyes and resting a bit would do her good. The sun blazed overhead. She brought her tulip closer and tried to cast a little shade with her skirt. Then she closed her eyes.

Forget Me Not

Then she heard a voice, hard to tell if it was a dream or real:

'Help me, I'm dying.'

Opening her eyes into a slit, she glanced at her tulip. No, it couldn't have been the tulip – who was still not breathing. Maybe she was already dead… a prospect that terrified Ida. Silently she recalled Tobar's tribute to the departed:

Time has wings,
So do people.
They both fly away
Freely.
Never forget,
Nothing ever vanishes;
Instead, everything
Comes to join us one day.

Nothing ever vanishes; instead, everything comes to join us one day.

She had no idea what else to do to settle herself down. Her exhausted body wouldn't let her get up. But the voice came again:

'Please oh please help. Or I'll die.'

It sounded like a young child. But they were on a mountainside. There was no one else around. Ida glanced around: all she could see, and as far as the eye could see, were the earth, the sky and white clouds. There were trees far in the distance, but that's not where the voice came from. It sounded much closer, and like someone much smaller. That's when Ida noticed it came from somewhere behind her. She turned a little and spotted a tiny sapling that had somehow pushed through a crack in the parched soil. She asked:

'Was that you? Asking for help?'

'Please,' replied the sapling, talking with great difficulty, 'Please give me a drop of water. Or I'll die.'

'OK,' said Ida, 'But I only have a few drops myself. My sick tulip and I also need water. Or we'll die too.'

'Please,' whined the sapling, 'I don't want to die. I'm too young yet.'

85

Aslı Eti

It was true. The sapling was still a child, and it shouldn't be left on this cracked earth on its own.

Would they ever be happy again if a young child died before their eyes – provided, that is, they lived that long! Of course not. 'If we're one short, we're incomplete,' Boika had said. If that sapling were to vanish, this mountain would also be incomplete. How can others be happy when there is sadness somewhere? Wouldn't that sadness eventually turn up where the happy were? Ultimately, yes. Ida thought she could see the smiling face of the storyteller shepherd and couldn't believe her eyes. His home was left so far behind them now... She felt she was in a dream as she thought all this, she felt she was looking at her own reflection on the glittering waters of the lake.

Suddenly she thought saw Patia, sitting with Jal, her interpreter:

'Your palms are filled with stars,' said Jal, this shows you're a kind person and you'll reach your goal.'

Ida asked, excited, 'Does that mean I get back home then?'

'You will reach your goal at the end of the journey, but your journey will not end,' replied Jal.

'How do you mean? I don't get it...' said Ida, looking puzzled.

'That's what she said,' replied Jal, adding, 'One drop can make a forest. She says you must never forget it.'

'I won't,' said Ida to herself, 'I won't...'

Ida lay exhausted, and her tulip was still not breathing. A dying sapling near her was pleading with her to survive. She opened her water bottle with trembling hands. She gave one drop to the sapling, one to her tulip and touched the last one to her lip. And suddenly it all grew dark.

She opened her eyes when heavy raindrops started wetting her face. It was bucketing down, yet the sun still shone. Ida was drenched, yet felt happy enough to smile. She drank her fill of the rainwater and looked at her tulip: breathing. Better than just breathing; she was clearly enjoying herself now, murmuring a little tulip song to herself in her velvety voice. They weren't dead, they were still living: this was unbelievable! Ida glanced at the sapling behind her, wondering if this

Forget Me Not

was a dream. No, the sapling was real, and it stood just where she'd looked for it. But its trunk looked much thicker and leaves much larger and glossier. The sapling was drinking its fill of the rainwater, and the more it did, the larger it grew.

Ida straightened up and asked:

'How did all this happen?'

The sapling replied cheerfully:

'You've saved my life. With that one drop you gave me… That's all I needed.'

'Really?' asked Ida, her eyes wide open in surprise. She wasn't dreaming or anything. That tiny sapling had grown and thrived in the course of one single day. The soil under their feet was no longer parched and cracked; with each new raindrop it burgeoned into fresh greenery.

'But one single drop… How can it change everything?'

'As you can see, it already has,' replied the sapling, sounding still quite upbeat, 'You've saved my life. I can't thank you enough.'

'You're welcome,' smile Ida, introduced her tulip and told the sapling about their journey.

'I can't believe you've picked her!' it scolded Ida, 'The girl who saved my life a moment ago can't be the same person as the one who'd picked this poor tulip!'

Ida bowed her head in shame. *How strange,* she thought, thinking of that moment on the path. The pesky girl insisting on picking the snow tulip could not have been the same one who was now cradling the tulip; she could not have been the same girl who had saved her own life, and the tulip's, and the sapling's.

No, those two were definitely not one and the same girl.

10

If you drop off the edge,
no one gives you a pair of wings.
You have to make your own.

One single drop of water that had revived the sapling had truly burgeoned into a forest. Patia's prophecy had come true. And thanks to this forest, Ida was able to find some water whenever she needed it in this hot and dry summer. Now a gentle breeze accompanied them up the slopes, shaded by trees and walking past young saplings. Ida thought all this might be the reward for making someone happy. As if the whole world had got together to help them in the driest spell of the summer. She thought happiness was something more than a trite word. It was simple and nice things. A drop of water and a song the tulip sang. Things like that.

On a glorious evening when entire sky was washed in myriad shades of pinks and purples by the setting sun, Ida and her tulip reached the base of the summit. It rose proudly only a few steps away, vanishing in the mists. But there it was. Just a little way ahead, no farther than an hour's trek.

Casting their minds back to a time four seasons ago, they wanted to pause briefly and relish their triumph. How distant the summit had looked when they were on the pasture with the storyteller shepherd, how unattainable! Recalled all that they had gone through just to get to this point. It really isn't as big as it looked, thought Ida, and the

Forget Me Not

shepherd had to be right: 'It obviously likes looking big though!' she said to her tulip with a smile. Her eyes were fixed on the misty top.

'Are you ready?' she asked, 'We'll be home tonight.'

It still seemed hard to believe. The mountain's peak was still a dream, too distant to thrill like a fortune that was promised but was nowhere near. So it would be impossible to believe they'd got there until she actually placed her foot on the summit. And anyway, when her tulip returned to her patch, they would be parted. Even the thought was enough to pain them both. This had been their struggle for weeks, no, months; and now that they were so close, why did they feel so strange? Every journey had – had to have - an end. Something had set them on their way, once they reached that something, their journey would naturally come to an end.

'Come along then,' said Ida, cradling the pot, 'Let's walk on. Soon we'll get there.'

The tulip sighed silently instead of replying. Ida began climbing over the rocks, keeping her eyes ahead as she tackled the steep slope. Without stopping or a break... Ignoring her tight chest and sweat breaking out on her forehead... Leaping from one steep boulder onto another...

Suddenly the ground moved under her. A few pebbles rolled downhill. Then a few larger stones. Ida gripped the rock she was standing on, she'd have stabbed it with her fingernails if she could, to save herself from plunging down the abyss under her feet. But the fall wouldn't stop; pebbles and stones and rocks rolled down into the abyss in a growing stream. It was a landslide.

Once the rumble stopped and things quietened down, Ida opened her eyes a crack. She was fine except for a few scratches on her arms and legs, and her tulip was also all right, her breathing regular. Just scared by the noise of the rocks, that's all. Ida straightened up slowly, careful not to disturb the stones. A deep, sheer drop had opened up at her feet. That must have been a thin layer of covering then, and it had given way to a gigantic drop when the rocks had rolled away. She had to cross this precipice to reach the summit. Or... she would

Aslı Eti

have to risk another four seasons to try to reach the summit from the other face. But they both knew all too well that the tulip wouldn't last that long.

Gone was that earlier proud bearing of triumphant warriors. Now they were two desperate wretches with colossal burdens on their shoulders, standing at the edge of a cliff. They had no idea what to do, or how to cross the abyss. The moon and the stars were taking over from the sinking sun. It would be impossible to carry on before morning. They obviously had to spend the night at the edge of the cliff.

'Impossible!' yelled Ida, 'Just as we'd got so far... It's impossible to cross this abyss.'

'Perhaps not,' suggested the tulip, 'Do you recall what the sage said?'

'No!' yelled Ida, glowering at the drop. There was nothing she wanted to think of, or recall. Looking at the precipice made her hair stand on end. All she wanted to do was to go to sleep and forget all this. But she did know she would wake up in the same place in the morning. She threw a tantrum as loud as she could. Then she fell totally silent.

Once she had calmed down, the tulip gently reminded her of the sage's words: 'Don't forget: no one gives you a pair of wings when you fall off the edge. You have to build your own.'

'Yeah, right!' interrupted Ida, 'So now we set about making wings, eh? No one and certainly no wings can make us fly over this abyss!'

They paused in the dark for a while. 'I wish I had some gift, like Mawa, Kafi and the others!' murmured Ida, 'Maybe then I would I could have saved us from the edge of this cliff...'

Just then, Kafi's skill in carpentry popped into her mind. He could make any tool or instrument. This gave her an idea. A simple one. She wasn't sure it would work, but trying *something* instead of sitting on her hands might be better at any rate. She looked around for some twigs, sticks and ivy. Surely the hands that had made a pair of sandals in a couple of hours could put together a bridge to cross this abyss, provided she had the right materials. And how was she going to secure

Forget Me Not

the bridge on the other side? She could tie a rope to the end, and try to loop it over one of the stunted trees on the other side; a much better option than swinging around the mountain in the other direction, and taking another four seasons to do so. All right, it wasn't a pair of wings, but a simple bridge could certainly do the job. And there wasn't anything else she could do anyway.

She wandered all night long in the light of the stars and the moon as she picked the materials for her bridge: dry twigs, sticks and ivy… She stacked it all by their camp and started weaving. She wove all night long and into the day. By the time she'd finished the long bridge, the sun was overhead.

Without a pause, she set about weaving the rope for the end since she wanted to reach the other side before dark. It was finished before sunset. She secured it to the bridge with a firm knot. All she needed now was a good throw to loop the rope over the bush opposite.

Her first attempts were unsuccessful. And the next… She just couldn't reach the bush. The rope either fell very close, or went too far; it occasionally slid over the bush and slipped free. She tried all day, and all night. The sun set again and rose again; it set once again and rose again. Ida wouldn't give up. She kept throwing the rope over to the other side. She could have given up and started walking in the other direction, but something inside kept telling her not to stop, to keep trying, even when she could barely lift her arms. The peak was so close, under her nose, close enough to touch; how could she possibly resign herself to giving up now?

It was in twilight, just before sunrise, when she finally looped the rope over the bush! She yelled, a cry of triumph that echoed around the mountain. Now there was nothing she could not do. She would cross that bridge over to the other side. She patted the invisible rope around her waist securely connecting her to the proud, unattainable, misty mountaintop, just as sure as Magariba and his star. No one could ever undo this fastening between them now. Ida knew that rope was there, and would never let them fall. After all they'd been through,

Aslı Eti

all those life and death situations: no rope would ever let Ida or her tulip fall. She was certain.

She had no intention of resting. She grabbed her tulip and stepped onto the bridge. The dry twigs crackled. Her eyes fixed on the other side, Ida stared ahead. Neither down, nor back. She walked. Without a pause, without thinking. Her steps firm. And only a few minutes later she reached the other side as if she'd been walking on the soft grass of a meadow. She wasn't surprised. She didn't rejoice. All she did was to turn round and yell at the cliff side she'd left just now:

'I don't need anyone else. I can build my own wings.'

11

No one is a hero in this world.
The way to happiness does not require heroics.

Ida and the tulip reached the summit in a flash. They looked down eagerly: there it was, their village! Ida's home, the tulip's soil, the path hidden in the greenery… everything was still there. All they had to do was to entrust themselves to the wind for the downhill slide. They were saved! In a few hours, the tulip would be back in her patch, and Ida on her way home.

Just as they were about to slide down, a muffled voice came from the mists surrounding the summit:

'Are you sure?'

A male voice. Ida swung around to look. She spotted a figure sitting in the mist. He must have been perched at the edge of the summit. She went over there, curious, still carrying her tulip.

It was a well-built, athletic gentleman of around forty or so. Judging by his clothes, backpack, rope and torch, he was an experienced mountaineer. But he was sitting at the edge of the sheer drop, feet hanging into the void.

'What are you doing here?' asked Ida, 'Why don't you get down?'

'I'm standing on the sky,' he replied, 'Right on top of the sea of clouds…'

Ida had never met any grown-up who spoke like that before; she couldn't help bursting into laughter.

Aslı Eti

'I'm sure no one else would have said that! You're weird…'

'So they say. No one had taken me seriously when I'd said I was going to climb to the summit too. All they did was call me weird.'

'But you've climbed, right?' asked Ida eagerly, 'Go down now so the celebrations can begin. Show them all you've made it.'

'I'm not really sure I want to go down though,' he replied, swinging his legs in the clouds, 'And I haven't the foggiest what to do once I get down, anyway.'

'Why?' asked Ida, sitting down beside him and hanging her legs over the edge. A shiver ran down the back of her neck all the way to her toes. It felt scary to lose contact with the ground under her feet.

'All I wanted was to reach this summit. I've made it… And I've been sitting down here all this time. Wondering what else I could do…'

'But you have made it!' exclaimed Ida, astonished, 'That wasn't easy at all; I know from personal experience. You're a hero. Doesn't that make you happy?'

'I'm no hero,' said the main, dejected.

'Go down, go back to your family, back home,' said Ida, sounding firmer, 'And tell them what you've achieved.'

'I've achieved nothing…'

'What do you mean? Of course you have. You've reached the summit, right?'

'Yes, but I've failed to do what I ought to have done instead. At the time, I was thinking all I had to do was to reach the summit. I was wrong.'

'How do you mean?' asked Ida.

'There was someone I had to save, but I couldn't,' he whispered, leaning down as far as he could from his seat and staring at the depths of the precipice. Ida thought he was about to let himself drop into the void. Thankfully he straightened up again at once.

He spoke of his best mate; they'd set off together. Just as they were about to reach the summit, there was a huge landslide.

'Rocks and stones were rolling down so fast… You wouldn't believe your eyes if you saw it!'

Forget Me Not

Ida's excitement deflated as his voice grew duller.

'He could be talking about what happened to us!' she whispered to her tulip. She was right; that was precisely what had happened to them a few days earlier. So summit landslides were regular events on this mountain.

'So what happened after the landslide?' she asked, intrigued about his way to the top. Had it been easier for him to cross the abyss, or harder?

'We struggled for days, and eventually found a gigantic tree trunk,' the mountaineer carried on, 'We rolled it all the way. It took days. And enormous hard work to lay it over the abyss. The idea was to walk over it to cross to the other side. My mate had a lot of stuff. I told him to leave it. He wouldn't listen. Said he'd never go without his stuff on his back.'

'So what did you do then?' asked Ida apprehensively. She could guess what came next, remembering how tiring it was to walk with all that heavy weight on her back. That weight must have created problems, she was sure.

'We stepped onto the log together. Took a few steps. At first everything was OK. But when we reached the middle, my mate suddenly lost his balance. I managed to grab his hand just as he was about to fall. I grabbed with all my might. "Don't worry, I won't let you go!" I said.'

Ida bowed her head; her eyes were welling up. She could feel her tulip trembling on her lap. 'Then?' she asked quietly.

'I held onto him for hours; I felt like I was dying, but I didn't let go. I was determined not to let go until my own arm was wrenched out of its socket. I pleaded for hours for someone to come to our help. No one came, no one heard me. Eventually my mate said he couldn't hold on any more. I told him to chuck his stuff; this would lighten the load on us both. "OK!" he said, tried to remove his backpack, but couldn't manage it. Then suddenly he let go of my hand. Or perhaps it just slipped. I don't know. But our eyes were locked as he fell down into the void.'

Aslı Eti

Ida and her tulip felt stunned as if this tragedy had happened to them personally. It wasn't long since they'd crossed that slender bridge… Ida thought she could never forgive herself if she'd dropped her tulip, a thought that made her feel the mountaineer's pain in her own heart.

'You're a kind man,' she said, 'You didn't sacrifice your mate just to save yourself. Which makes you a kind man. And Patia had said kind people always reach their goal. She always knows the future.'

'I don't know Patia,' replied the mountaineer in his dull voice, 'And I have no idea what my purpose is. I'll sit here for a while.'

'But you're all on your own here,' said Ida dolefully. No one should stay alone at the edge of a precipice. It was a heart-breaking sight.

'You're just sitting there, looking down. Wouldn't it be better to come down with us? Something totally unexpected might happen, who knows?'

'Thanks for the offer, but I can't. There's nothing down there that could make me happy.'

'How do you know?' murmured Ida. She couldn't just leave him there and carry on. Something inside told her not to leave him alone. Everyone they'd met on this journey had offered help of a sort; so now she could do the same for the mountaineer. She told him about her journey. She explained her first goal was to take her sick tulip back, since this was the only way the tulip could get better. The next thing was for Ida to go home. Only then would she stop feeling guilty. Why didn't he do the same? Why didn't he leave his stuff here and just go down? Sitting here wasn't going to bring his mate back. Just like the sage who lived in the cave and who couldn't bring Lea back. She told the mountaineer about the sage and the healing stone he had forgotten under the bricks. Perhaps the mountaineer had also forgotten or lost something under the ice or in the snow at the base of the mountain? The landslide had also carried the winter snows down into the abyss; perhaps the mountaineer had to go and find whatever it was that was buried under the ice? She offered to help with his search:

96

Forget Me Not

'I can help, you know. Maybe you have to look under the ice, right at the bottom of the precipice.'

'Even if you're right… It's not easy going down there,' lamented the mountaineer.

'But you don't have to go down at all!' interjected Ida, sounding quite confident, 'If we can melt the snow, you will be able to see what it is from here.'

'All right,' said the mountaineer. Since there was nothing else he could do, he wasn't going to lose anything by trying.

It took them all day, but they wove long ropes of ivy, tied them to gigantic torches of twigs tied to long sticks, lit a fire by rubbing dry sticks together, and lowered these torches down into the abyss.

The torches lit up the night on their way down, sparks flying here and there. Whatever had been frozen out of sight in the ice would be revealed when daylight came.

Ida and the mountaineer held the ropes as if they were fishing in a frozen lake, their lines hanging into the abyss… They sat, their feet dangling over the void, and the torches lighting up the bottom. Ida kept her tulip on her lap all night long. She had no intention of letting go of her friend, even for a moment as they sat so close to this terrifying precipice.

It was a long night. It felt as if the sun would never rise. The torches needed to be lit again and again. Ida didn't get tired of sending the torches down, all the way down to the bottom. She grabbed the thick ropes tight, ignoring the pain in her slender fingers. She watched the sparks all night long without blinking.

At long last the sun rose. Exhausted, Ida and the mountaineer pulled their torches back up. They peered over the edge curiously, trying to see beyond the layer of clouds, trying to see what lay under the ice at the bottom. It came into view once the mists began to disperse.

The mountaineer stared and stared. It was an old pair of binoculars! Something he had been carrying ever since he was a child, something he had quite forgotten about. A present from his father,

Aslı Eti

who had told him about their magic power to bring close what lay in the distance. They reminded the mountaineer why he had wanted to climb to the top.

'If I could climb to the very top, I could see the whole world, and then choose where I wanted to go.'

'Great!' said Ida.

'What I need is those binoculars... I must get down to retrieve them.'

They knew this was dangerous. They also knew equally well that he had to do it.

'All I have to do is drive a sturdy piton here. I'll lash my rope securely and climb down. Child's play for a experienced mountaineer like me...'

(*A piton,* thought Ida, *That must be what a mountaineer calls his spike.*)

It had to be. Nothing was impossible for a mountaineer who'd made it to the top. In fact, everything was possible once you wanted it.

'Do you want us to come along?' asked Ida.

'No, no. Your flower can't take it. And you've already helped enough. The rest is up to me now.'

'I'm really curious where you'll go next,' said Ida with a smile.

'I'll soon find out!' said the mountaineer, and carried on. 'The only thing I can't believe is... my goal was to reach this summit; I spent years to make it happen. And yet all I had to do was to go to the bottom of the ravine!'

He followed with a guffaw at himself:

'I could have sat here for forty years, and it would never have occurred to me!'

He was right. He might never have found those binoculars, because he didn't even know they were there. So sometimes instead of just sitting and waiting, you had to gather the courage to get up and look for something.

Ida and the tulip took their leave of the mountaineer, wishing one another luck as they hugged. Would they every meet again? *Who*

Forget Me Not

knows? thought Ida. All she knew was she would never forget him. Just like all the other friends she had made on this journey, even though they might look like they were slipping away from her fingers, in actual fact none was ever lost. They would stay friends for ever, tied as they were with that invisible rope in Magariba's dream. At least Ida thought so: the storyteller shepherd, the tall tree in the forest, Jal, Patia, the sage, Magariba and the other boys… and now the mountaineer, who was driving his piton into the cliff edge.

Once he'd fed the rope the piton, he waved at Ida and the tulip, let himself down the cliff. They waved back. They had struggled so hard to reach the top, just like the mountaineer. And now it was time for them to go down too.

12

You never come back the same as you start out.

Ida clutched her tulip and slid down the hill. They glided from the peak, amongst the clouds hanging in the air and the mist clinging to the slopes. They were in an indescribable state of euphoria that comes from having completed a seemingly impossible journey. Even the wind was helping them now, a gentle tail wind that speeded them up. They descended in total silence. Either they were unwilling to break the magic of the moment, or they had no idea what to say to each other. They might not have yet admitted it, but getting back also meant separation.

At long last they reached their homeland. There they were, right on that hidden path. The tulip's own soil was waiting for them at the end. They couldn't believe they were back. As if they'd got to these lands through a time tunnel.

The tulip took deep breaths of the village air.

'I missed it so much!' she exclaimed with bittersweet job.

'See, you're already feeling better, right? You seem to be breathing more easily. You're perking up, aren't you?'

'Yes,' said the tulip, breathing deeply the air of her own soil. She was staring around as if she would never see this place again, as if she didn't want to miss a single moment. Ida was carrying her home at a trot now.

Soon they reached the tulip's patch. They felt the ground under

Forget Me Not

their feet, as if they could sense its breathing. They now stood at the exact spot Ida had picked the tulip four seasons ago. They hugged tight. Or rather, Ida was hugging the flowerpot, and the tulip was nuzzling Ida's cheek. Ida didn't want to let go of her tulip ever again. She thought she couldn't survive without her friend. What she wanted most was to take the tulip to her own home. She loved her too much to ever let go.

She stood there motionless for a few minutes. But then she thought this would have been no different from the selfishness that had picked the tulip months earlier. Yet the girl who had picked the tulip and the one hugging her tight now were not one and the same. What she had to do was to replant her tulip at once. As soon as possible. That was the only way to revive the tulip fully, and to make sure the foretold rebirth came about.

She gave the tulip's slender stem a gentle kiss. She then began digging. She dug until she'd reached a depth that would give the tulip a comfortable home with enough nutrients. Planting the tulip carefully, she patted the soil over the roots.

The tulip looked around curiously.

'It's all changed,' she said with a smile, 'I don't recognise many, but we're neighbours. I'm sure we'll introduce ourselves.'

None of the plants nearby even turned for a quick glance at the tulip, probably because she was all skin and bones, all her petals gone, just a bald stem. Without her old enchanting beauty, there was naturally none of the attention she had once taken for granted. No one had recognised the old fabulous beauty, the adored snow tulip of long ago. Some even looked disturbed by her arrival. She decided to ignore the whispers carried on the breeze.

'We'll get used to one another in time,' she said to Ida.

Although she didn't want to upset Ida, she hadn't been able to hide the trembling in her voice.

'Of course you will. Just don't worry... And you'll soon perk up, and soon be as beautiful as before. I'm going to stay here, beside you, until I see you get better.'

Aslı Eti

The tulip didn't reply. After a brief silence, she said:

'You're tired though. Better go without further delay. I'll be fine, don't worry.'

'No,' interjected Ida, 'Don't insist, all right? I'm not going anywhere until I see you get better.'

No amount of pleading could convince Ida to go back. She sat down and started waiting, chatting and singing to cheer up her tulip. The sun was about to set, but there was no visible improvement.

Eventually the tulip said in a shaky voice:

'I have something to tell you.'

'Of course,' said Ida, 'You know you can tell me anything.'

'Somewhere deep inside,' the tulip started, paused, and carried on, 'Somewhere deep inside there's something I've been hiding. Something I don't want to tell you. I mean, I didn't, but now I have to.'

'You've lost me,' said Ida, confused about what the tulip meant to say; she could sense, though, that she wasn't going to enjoy what she was about to hear. She was filled with a strange fear, one that recognised. Just like the time she was about to lose her tulip in the depths of the forest.

'Just like the mountaineer hiding something at the bottom of the precipice,' said the tulip, bowing her head, 'I'm also hiding something inside, right at the bottom.'

'What is it? What are you hiding?' asked Ida anxiously.

'I'll never be the same again,' replied the tulip quietly.

'How? How do you mean you'll never be the same again?'

'I just won't be the same again, that's all. I'll never be a glorious snow tulip like I was before. Even if I am now back in my patch.'

Ida couldn't believe her ears. How was this possible? How would the tulip cope? And why had she never mentioned it right at the start? Was everything a huge lie then, just a fabrication presented to her as a prophecy, the journey's end, the promised rebirth: all that, just a huge lie? Did it even matter that they'd completed this journey? Nothing or no one could console her, Ida thought. But what she wanted was not consolation. She wanted the truth.

Forget Me Not

'At first I wanted to get back,' explained the tulip, 'I fooled myself into believing I'd be the same again if I went back. What else could I do?'

Ida cringed so much, she felt so weary after all that had happened that she placed her head on her knees, clutching her head. She shut her eyes shut and sat still for a while.

'Everything would be better if I could get back to my patch. That's what I thought at first. But I always secretly knew I'd never be the same again.'

The tulip was speaking non-stop now; it must feel good to finally let it all out. She carried on:

'You had to get back home. You had to cross the mountain, and the only way you could do that was if you took me back to my patch, at least according to the prophecy. I knew I would never be the same though, but I shut up, just didn't tell you this simple fact. What else could I do? Either I would perish someplace all on my own, or I would come with you. I chose to come with you. This way, I wouldn't hold you back, and I could dream of seeing my patch again...'

Ida tried to speak, struggling to get the words out past the lump in her throat:

'I'm sorry,' was all she could manage as the tears began streaming down her cheeks.

'Please don't cry. I'm not cross with you. I'd forgiven you long ago. Remember that night when you refused to give me to Fifika?'

'Yes.'

'You're my friend,' whispered the tulip, trying to comfort Ida, 'You can't stay cross with your friend, can you?'

Ida didn't know what to say: she had ruined the tulip's life, yet the tulip was now trying to console *her*. In that velvety singsong voice, selflessly consoling Ida.

'And after all those dangers we've faced, I don't regret this journey at all. If I had stayed, would I ever have seen all those wonders? Heard Lea's song or Jal's music? Just think... Would I now tell you about all this if I had never seen or heard them, or learnt about them? If my

Aslı Eti

eyes, ears and heart were ignorant of what I know now, I'd never have said any of it.'

Ida apologised over and over again, saying she would regret what she'd done for as long as she lived.

'Go on, leave me now,' whispered the tulip, 'Go now. I've missed my place; it will do me good to rest in my patch.'

'Where will I go?' asked Ida, her eyes red with crying.

'Home, of course. Where you belong.'

'I'll be alone there,' said Ida; she was panting, trying to gather her strength at every word so she could complete the sentence. 'I'll have no one to talk to. And no one would believe me anyway if I told my story. I mean, I don't even know if I can call it home now.'

'But remember,' interrupted the tulip, 'That's what you were saying right at the start; that's exactly how you felt then. You were so hopeless and lonely… But now you know you're neither. You're never going to be the same either. Just like me. And maybe it's not a bad thing, for me not to be the same as before. Neither you, nor I can ever be the same as before now.'

She was right; neither could go back to her old self now. But was the place they called home really still home? Ida felt like the mountaineer who had been sitting at the peak once he'd got there. He had reached the end of the road, but had no idea what to do next. What he felt was as sharp as and agonising as an ache, and whatever it was called, it stood right in the middle of a void as dark as the darkest night.

13

Loneliness is desperately wanting to go back home and realising it's no longer there.

Soon night would turn into day. It was pitch black; you couldn't see your hand in front of your face. The tulip still kept begging Ida to go home, and Ida still resisted, waiting by her friend, scared of getting lost again, of never being able to find her way again. She wasn't even sure she knew where her home was. Patia's words kept echoing in her mind:

'You will reach your goal at journey's end, but your journey won't be over.'

So Patia must have known then what would happen. Jal was right; Patia definitely saw the future. Ida wished she'd understood it then, wished she'd understood what Patia said in that first moment. But that's not how the world worked. It didn't use words to communicate with people. Or perhaps it used easily understood words, but people just failed to hear, see or understand.

The tulip had been sleeping deeply for hours. She looked peaceful; her breathing was regular in the silence, as if her roots grasped the soil a little more firmly. Ida couldn't take her eyes off the tulip: even without a single petal left, even as a scrawny twig, the flower still managed to fill her heart with an indescribable happiness.

The sun rose as Ida was still pondering. The tulip opened her eyes with the first light of day, took a deep breath as she did every morning and released a single crystal clear teardrop. And that's when it all

Aslı Eti

happened! The moment the teardrop hit the soil, the graceful stem suddenly drew itself upright and reached towards the sky. Then four blood red flowers suddenly bloomed on new branches! One for each season of her journey. Their heads were bowed, facing the ground and not the sky, their eyes fixed on the soil. So vibrant a red that they might have been painted in blood like a memento of that extraordinary journey! The tulip looked totally different from all the flowers the world had ever seen before.

Touching the blossoms gingerly, Ida whispered:

'You're the loveliest and the saddest flower in the world.'

'Thanks to you,' said the tulip with a smile in her velvety voice.

Ida kept silent, not knowing what to say: could you really owe new birth or a new lease of life to someone who'd crushed and annihilated you?

It was finally time for her to go home.

'I'm scared,' she said in a trembling voice.

'It won't be the same this time, you know,' murmured the tulip, 'Now that you know it's all up to you...'

'It's all up to me,' repeated Ida. She repeated it silently so as not to forget. *It's all up to me.*

The tulip kept whispering, dozens of words circling in Ida's mind. They reminded her not to forget.

'No one can stop you. Remember the moment you crossed the bridge on your own and reached the summit. Don't forget you have wings.'

Ida recalled her own words echoing on the rocks of the pinnacle:

'I don't need anyone else. I can build my own wings.'

'Do you remember what Patia said?' continued the tulip, 'Your hands are filled with stars. You're kind hearted. You'll definitely reach your goal and attain whatever it is your heart desires...'

'I won't forget,' said Ida as she set off, constantly reminding herself that they were tied for ever by an invisible and untouchable rope.

Forget Me Not

'Don't forget,' repeated the tulip quietly, 'Nothing happens unless you dream of it. Don't forget.'

Ida shut her eyes tight and repeated over and over.

'I won't forget, I won't forget, I won't forget…'

14

Note from Ida:
You may think you'll understand it all when you grow up.
Instead you'll even forget what you know.
Growing up is like falling into a deep sleep…

I should never have forgotten…
　I had promised myself, and my tulip too…
　I wasn't going to forget.
　Never.
　But I failed.
　I couldn't keep my promise. I forgot everything.
　It's all my fault, I know. I can only blame one person, only share my guilt with one person.
　The present me.
　The person that emerged as I grew up is completely different from me. She's just pretending to be me. She's confounding me and making me forget things I know best.
　In other words, where I thought I would understand everything when I grew up, I ended up forgetting even the things I knew.
　It's been such a long time since my journey. And I found myself alone on these lands I thought of as home, unable to know what I want, what I have to do or wait for in this world.
　Thankfully that old, dusty book turned up and reminded me of

Forget Me Not

the tale I'd forgotten. That's why I told it today. For myself. So I could recall whatever I had forgotten.

My name is Ida.

One day, a long, long time ago, in a land far, far away, I set out on a journey most of you might find incredible.

My whole world changed beyond my wildest imaginings when I set my heart on a snow tulip. I discovered another world beyond the one I knew; in fact, I was thrown into that world headfirst. All on my own.

To be fair, I shouldn't say all on my own. It would cut my old friend the tulip to the quick if she ever heard.

I wonder where she is now, and if she can hear me. Could she possibly know that I've told the story?

Could a tulip really hear you?

Of course she can.

I know most of you don't believe me.

No one believed me then either, at the end, when I reached the journey's end. No matter what I said or did, I failed to convince a single person. An irritating smile would appear on faces, and I would face the same foolish questions time and time again, as if they were all in cahoots. I felt as if I were constantly trying to prove a lie. At first I kept answering tirelessly, but I eventually realised that it was useless... And I gave up trying to convince people. Perhaps that's why even I had forgotten it all. As I had said right at the start, it's only now I recall I had forgotten... I wasn't even aware that I had forgotten at the time.

If you want to know what happened to my tulip, read on: she is reborn every year through the snow to herald the arrival of spring. Her blossoms still look down, and she still waters the soil with her dewdrop tears every morning at daybreak. To remind us that the beauty of the world we might think we've lost for ever actually sticks around to urge us to preserve it for ever. She wishes that anyone who can see her would use not only eyes but also hearts to see her. Today the *Fritillaria imperialis* is known as the Weeping Bride, or Anatolian Tulip, Upside-down Tulip or Crown Imperial.

Aslı Eti

Neither of us stayed as we once were. That is precisely why I had to recollect this tale.

It's only natural for me to suffer if I can't think about it, or recall it, or even fail to think; if I am so lost.

But getting lost is the last thing to do once you've remembered what you'd forgotten.

Quite the opposite… If you can find the As-yet-unnamed-You somewhere, then you'll know what to do in this world. Then you can choose your own favourite name for yourself. Yes, yes, just like little Magariba…

If one more person found happiness with his or her star in the sky every day, and left even the most striking beauty in its place, laying aside selfishness, the world would get better. It is that simple. And don't forget, if someone somewhere is sad, that sorrow will ultimately touch you too…

Now that I recall it all, I also know what to do.

I now know that the simplest truths are the least well known, that they are the ones that are forgotten first.

That not even the highest mountain is as big as we might think…

That a single drop of water can give birth to a forest, and that everything is possible in the world…

That the departed eventually join us; that nothing is ever lost…

That kindness and beauty are infinite…

And that nothing happens unless I dream of it…

I know exactly what I have to do.

Just like the sage who lifted the bricks, and the mountaineer who descended to the bottom of the ravine to retrieve his binoculars, I'm going to find my tulip again.

I'm sure she's still there, in her patch, waiting in silence for my return.

THE END

About the Author

Aslı Eti

Born on 11 May 1978 in Istanbul, Turkey, Aslı Eti holds a BA in Social Sciences and Philosophy from Bosphorus University. After fifteen years of managing global brands in multinational advertising agencies, she finally took the plunge to pursue her wild dream of writing. Her début novel *Forget Me Not*, published in June 2016, became an instant bestseller in Turkey with five reprints in its first year alone and even found its way into school curriculums.

Her second novel *Fourteen Days of the World* followed a year later, and a 'Philosophy for Children' short story series called *School of Wisdom* came in 2018.

Aslı Eti is committed to inspiring journeys of self-discovery. Fully convinced of the healing power of words, she is passionate about motivating people of all ages to seek the purpose of their lives, to reclaim their own power and to illuminate the world.

Feyza Howell

Armed with a BA (Hons.) in Graphic Design, Feyza Howell has worked in design, advertising, TV production, marketing, product management and business development in several countries across the world. Throughout this time she has always drawn, written and translated. Resolving to help bring great literature to a wider audience, she has ultimately exchanged international business for translation and writing full time.

Feyza Howell lives in Berkshire, where she draws, teaches dance, translates, and writes punchy stories that she might publish one day.

Printed in the United States
By Bookmasters